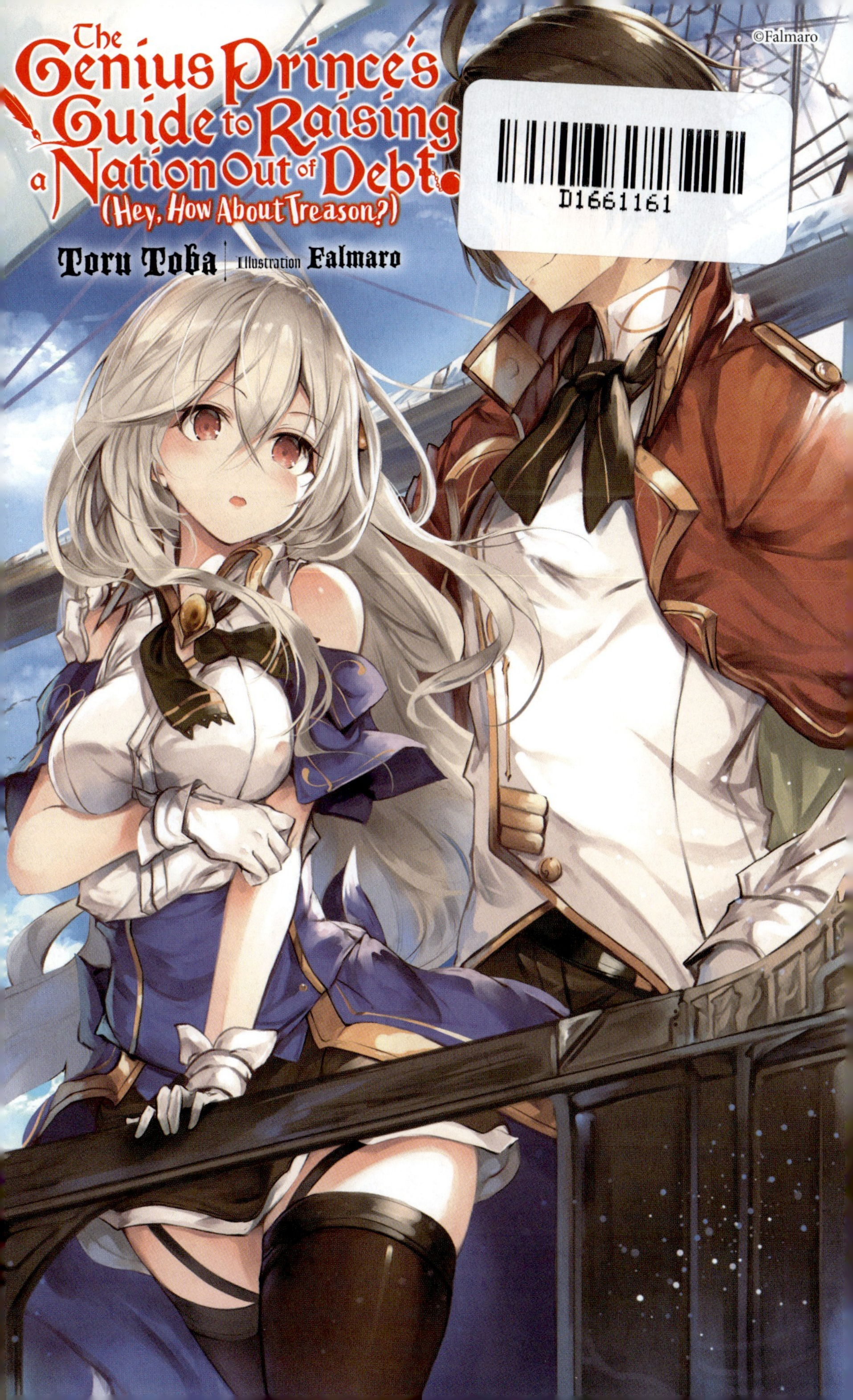
©Falmaro
The Genius Prince's Guide to Raising a Nation Out of Debt
(Hey, How About Treason?)
Toru Toba
Illustration Falmaro

Crown Princess of Natra

Falanya

"I bet Wein is having a ball under puffy white clouds and sailing over the deep blue sea!"

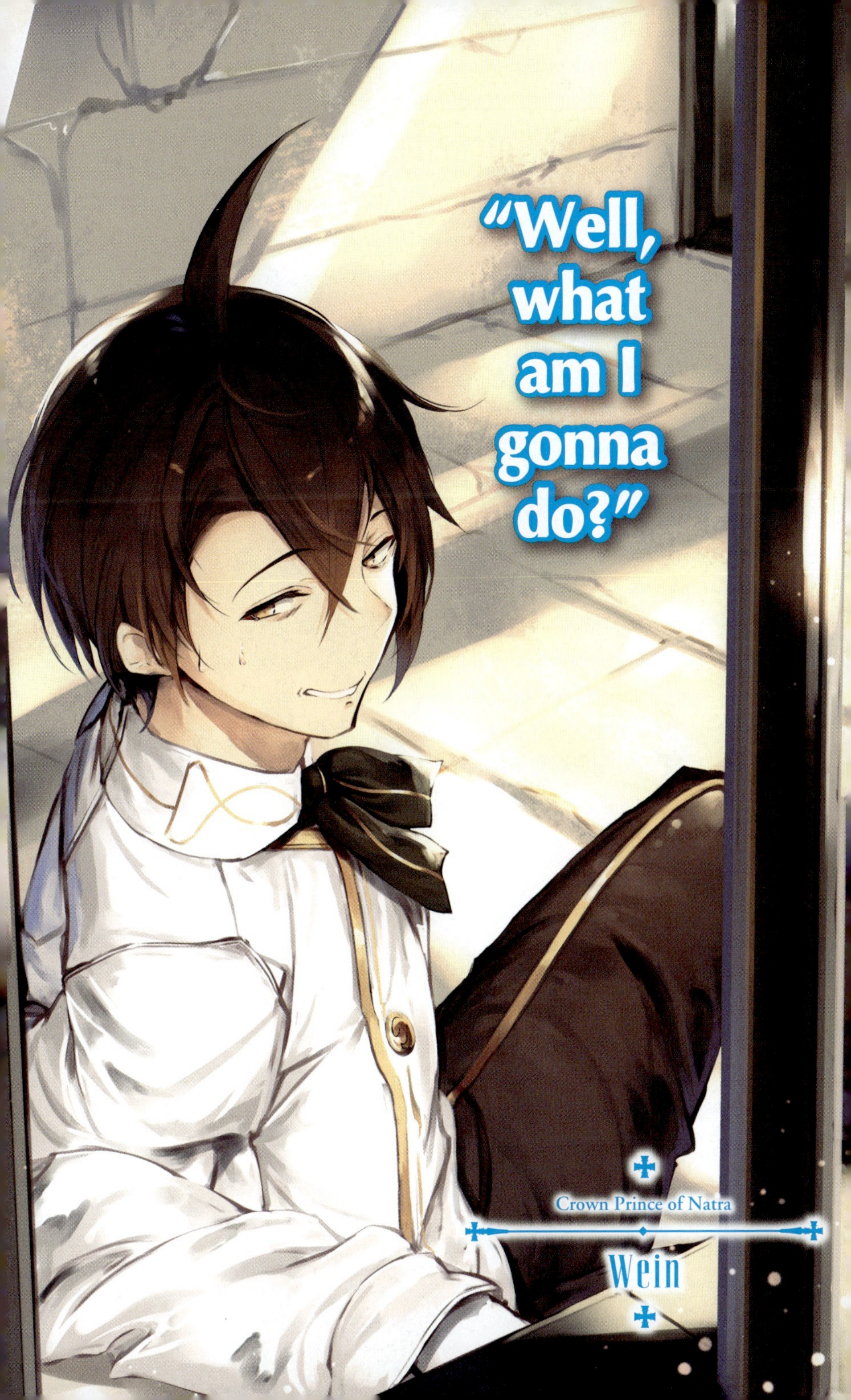
"Well, what am I gonna do?"
Crown Prince of Natra
Wein

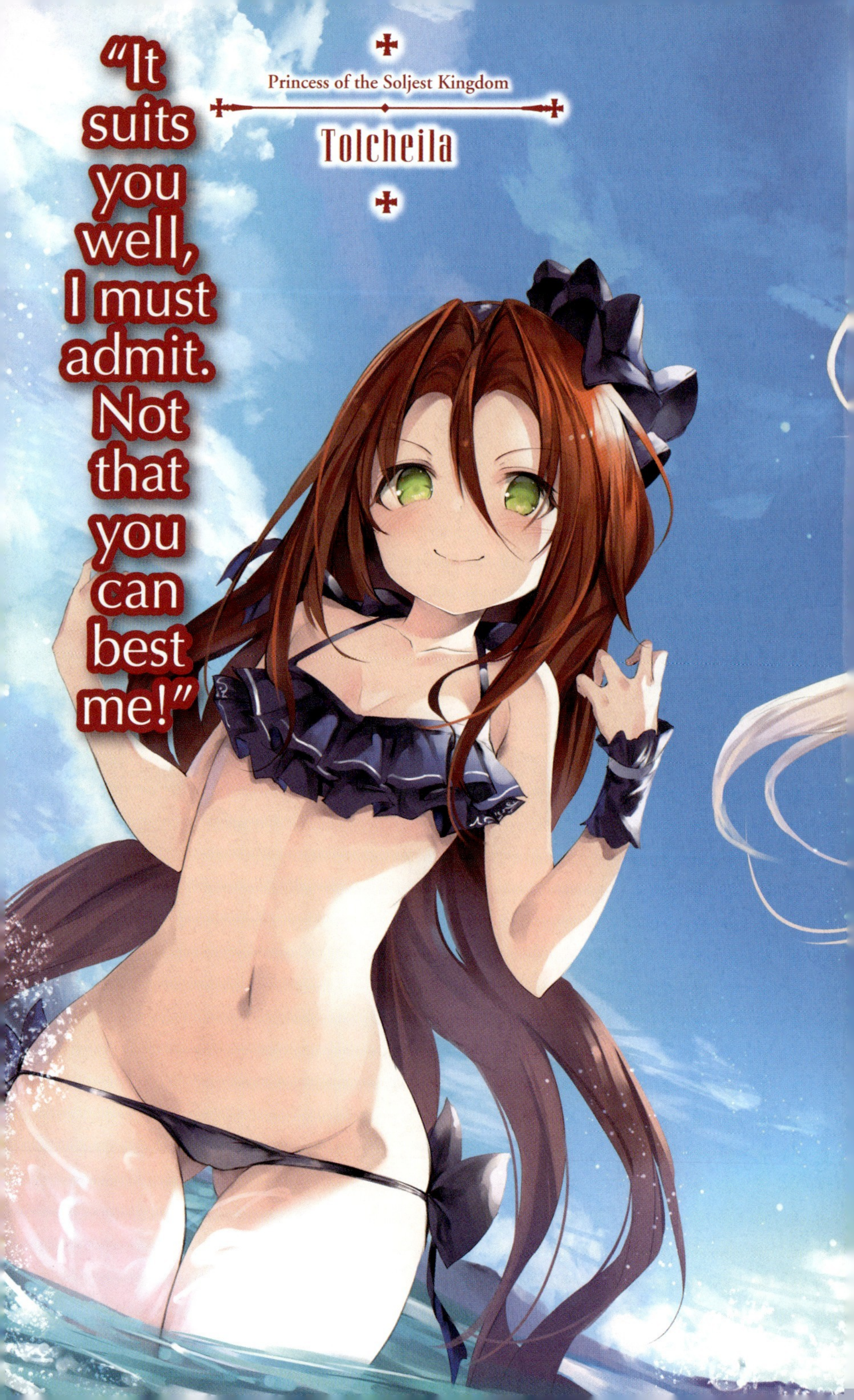

"It suits you well, I must admit. Not that you can best me!"
Princess of the Soljest Kingdom
Tolcheila

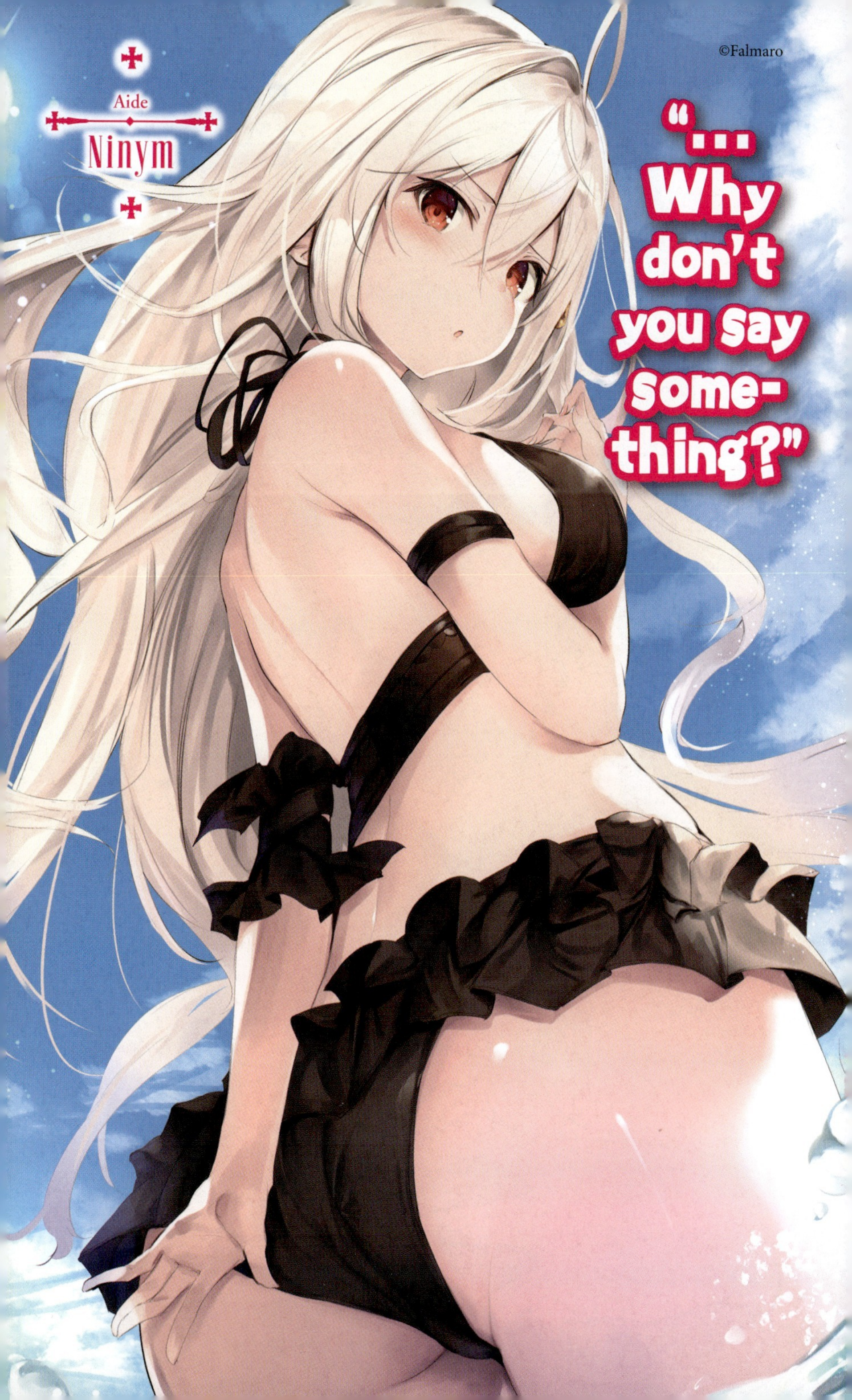

Aide
Ninym
©Falmaro
"... Why don't you say some-thing?"

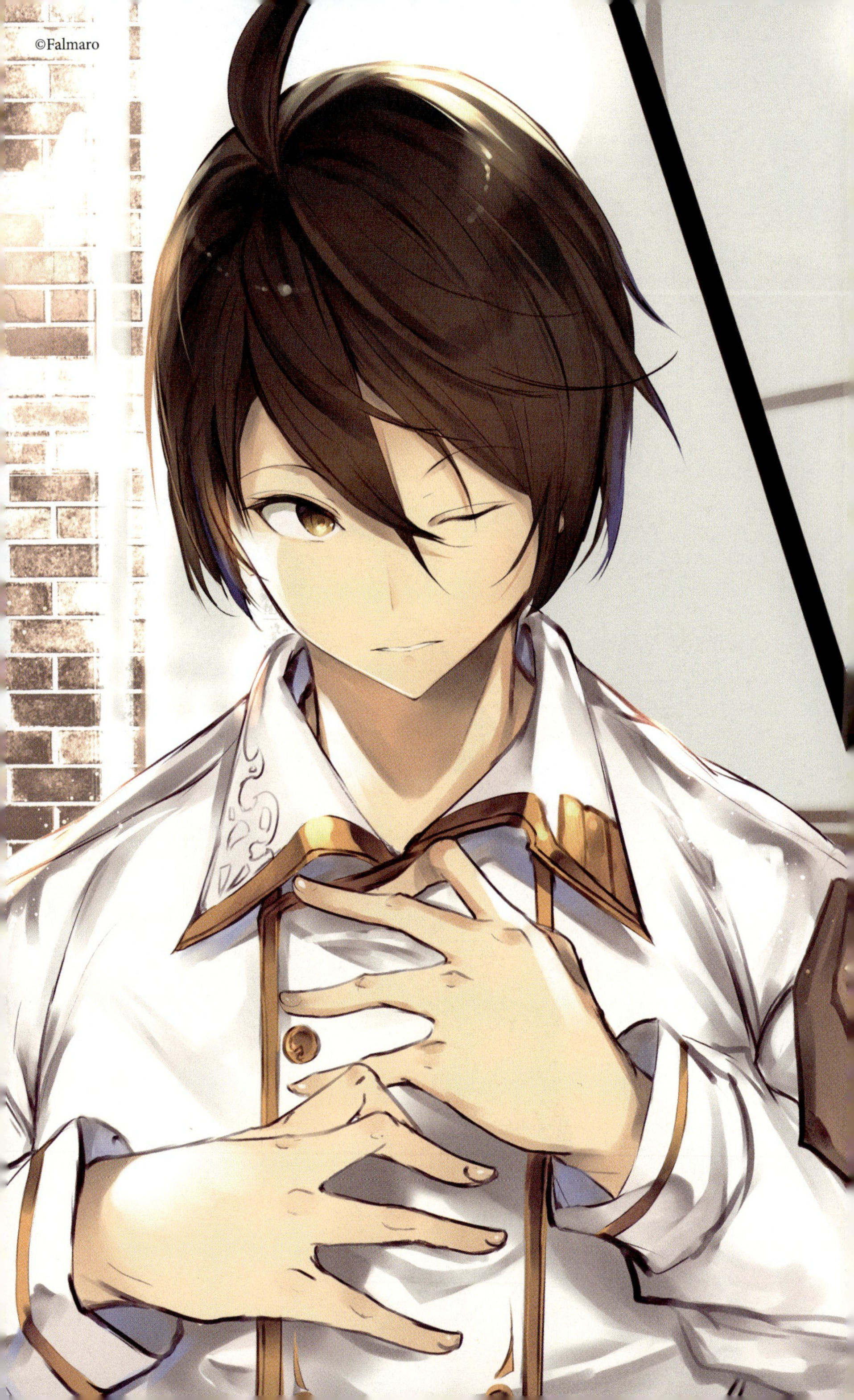
©Falmaro

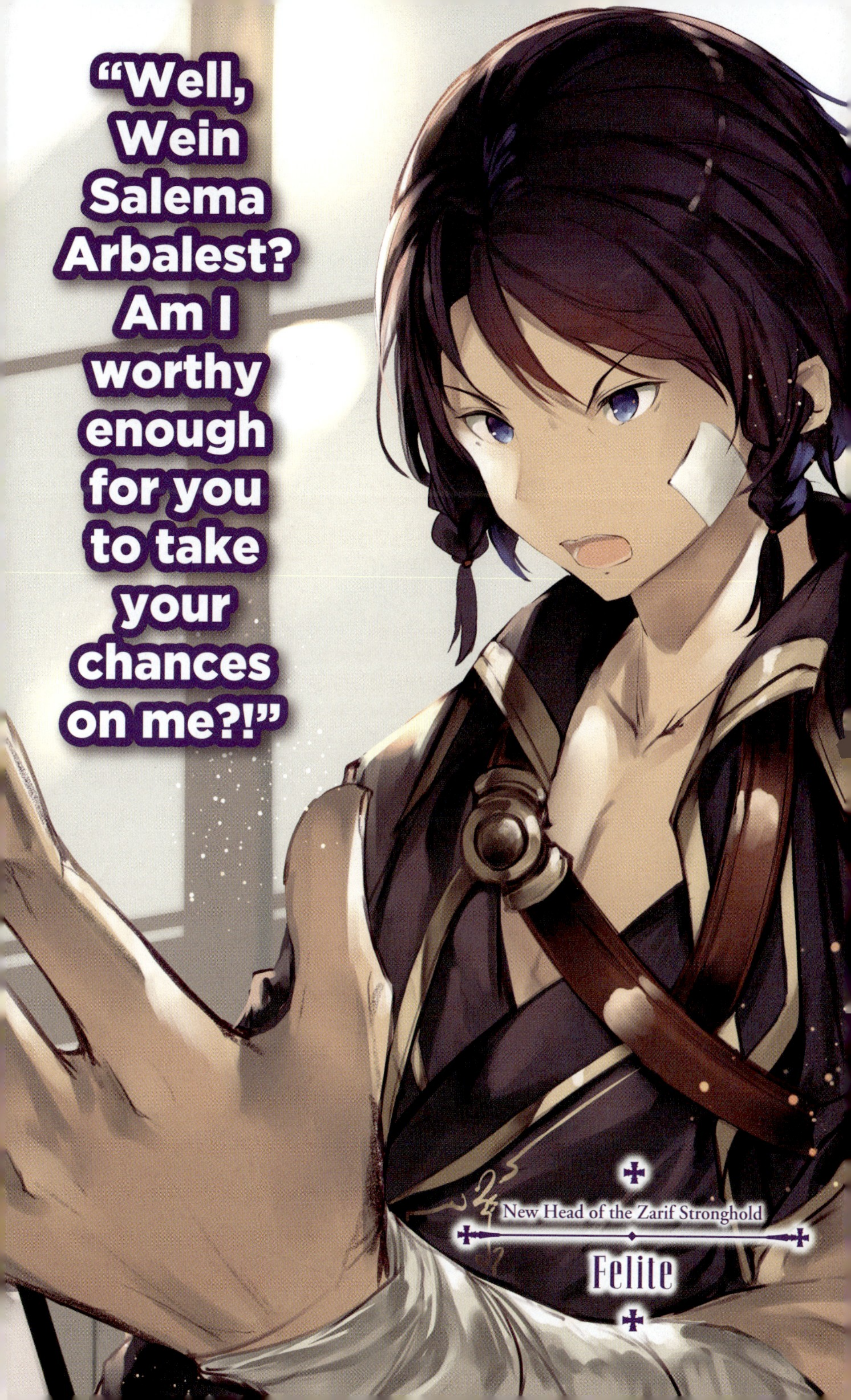
"Well, Wein Salema Arbalest? Am I worthy enough for you to take your chances on me?!"
New Head of the Zarif Stronghold
Felite

CONTENTS

The Genius Prince's Guide to Raising a Nation Out of Debt (Hey, How About Treason?)

Chapter 1
Hey, How About Heading South?
1

Chapter 2
From Surprise Incident to Surprise Meeting
13

Chapter 3
Rainbow Crown
49

Chapter 4
The Loss of Legends
95

Chapter 5
At the End of a Rainbow
135

Epilogue
157

©Falmaro

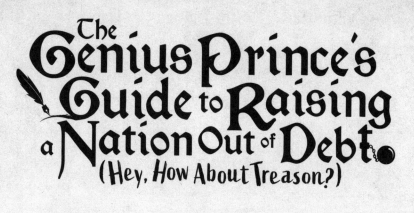

Toru Toba
Illustration **Falmaro**

New York

The Genius Prince's Guide to Raising a Nation Out of Debt. (Hey, How About Treason?)

6

Toru Toba

Translation by Jessica Lange
Cover art by Falmaro

This book is a work of fiction. Names, characters, places, and incidents are the product of the author's imagination or are used fictitiously. Any resemblance to actual events, locales, or persons, living or dead, is coincidental.

TENSAI OUJI NO AKAJI KOKKA SAISEI-JYUTSU ~ SOUDA, BAIKOKU SHIYOU ~ volume 6
Copyright © 2020 Toru Toba
Illustrations copyright © 2020 Falmaro
All rights reserved.
Original Japanese edition published in 2020 by SB Creative Corp.

This English edition is published by arrangement with SB Creative Corp., Tokyo in care of Tuttle-Mori Agency, Inc., Tokyo.

English translation © 2021 by Yen Press, LLC

Yen Press, LLC supports the right to free expression and the value of copyright. The purpose of copyright is to encourage writers and artists to produce the creative works that enrich our culture.

The scanning, uploading, and distribution of this book without permission is a theft of the author's intellectual property. If you would like permission to use material from the book (other than for review purposes), please contact the publisher. Thank you for your support of the author's rights.

Yen On
150 West 30th Street, 19th Floor
New York, NY 10001

Visit us at yenpress.com
facebook.com/yenpress
twitter.com/yenpress
yenpress.tumblr.com
instagram.com/yenpress

First Yen On Edition: April 2021

Yen On is an imprint of Yen Press, LLC.
The Yen On name and logo are trademarks of Yen Press, LLC.

The publisher is not responsible for websites (or their content) that are not owned by the publisher.

Library of Congress Cataloging-in-Publication Data
Names: Toba, Toru, author. | Falmaro, illustrator. | Lange, Jessica (Translator), translator.
Title: The genius prince's guide to raising a nation out of debt (hey, how about treason?) / Toru Toba ; illustration by Falmaro ; translation by Jessica Lange.
Other titles: Tensai ouji no akaji kokka saisei-jyutsu, souda, baikoku shiyou. English
Description: First Yen On edition. | New York, NY : Yen On, 2019-
Identifiers: LCCN 2019017156| ISBN 9781975385194 (v. 1 : pbk.) | ISBN 9781975385170 (v. 2 : pbk.) | ISBN 9781975309985 (v. 3 : pbk.) | ISBN 9781975310004 (v. 4 : pbk.) | ISBN 9781975313708 (v. 5 : pbk.) | ISBN 9781975319830 (v. 6 : pbk.)
Subjects: LCSH: Princes—Fiction.
Classification: LCC PL876.O25 T4613 2019 | DDC 895.6/36—dc23
LC record available at https://lccn.loc.gov/2019017156

ISBNs: 978-1-9753-1983-0 (paperback)
       978-1-9753-1984-7 (ebook)

10 9 8 7 6 5 4 3 2 1

LSC-C

Printed in the United States of America

The Genius Prince's Guide to Raising a Nation Out of Debt
(Hey, How About Treason?)

WESTERN KINGDOMS
EARTHWORLD EMPIRE
THE GIANT'S BACKBONE
PATURA ISLANDS
ZARIF STRONGHOLD
SOUTH SEA

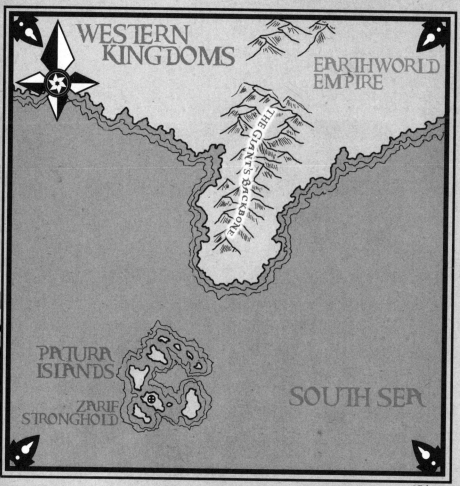

Chapter 1 | Hey, How About Heading South?

Spring.

Three summers had passed since the crown prince had been appointed regent of the Kingdom of Natra.

The days had been rocky. Ever since the death of the Emperor of Earthworld, the ruler of Eastern Varno, trouble had crashed into Natra like waves.

Future historians would certainly be rendered slack-jawed by the never-ending trials and tribulations targeting the kingdom.

In the next breath, they would praise Natra for knocking back each one.

Natra overcame. Once the subject of ridicule, the poor runt of a kingdom had managed to blow back every challenge to come its way.

The one who led the people during the era termed the Great War of Kings was Wein Salema Arbalest, fated to be remembered by historians.

Sensible internal policies. The proactive eagerness to step into the battlefield as needed. The devilish cunning to toy with neighboring nations. The benevolence to put his people first.

He was the perfect prince.

The prince was the key to Natra's future. Bathed in the warm spring sun, the citizens were certain of this fact.

However…the sky was bound to cloud over, even in the most blessed of lands.

In fact, a spring storm was brewing in Willeron Palace in the Kingdom of Natra.

"Nghhhhhh."

Currently sulking; approach at your own risk, warned the look on a girl's face as she sat on the bed with a big pout.

Falanya Elk Arbalest. Wein's younger sister and the crown princess of Natra.

Though she'd been young when Wein ascended to the post of regent, she'd recently started acting like a real adult, maturing in mind and body…

…Except now. She was in the middle of a childish tantrum.

"How much longer are you going to sulk, Falanya?"

A boy with red eyes and a head of white hair—a Flahm—sighed loudly.

His name was Nanaki Ralei, and he was Falanya's appointed servant. His attitude toward the crown princess might be considered rude to some, but as they were childhood friends, it didn't bother either of them.

"…I'm not sulking." Falanya turned the other way with a huff.

"You are."

"Am not."

"Are too."

"AM! NOT!" Falanya snapped back, but that didn't seem to faze Nanaki.

"Throw a fit—see if I care—but you need to pull yourself together when you're in public. You're worrying the officials."

"*Gulp.*" He'd gotten her weak spot. She knew what he was talking about.

From some topographic, cultural, or national influence, the royal family was generally imperturbable. The current crop of rulers was no exception: King Owen, Prince Wein, Princess Falanya, even the dearly departed queen.

It was extremely rare for any of them to lash out at the officials in sadness or anger.

This was exactly why the officials were thrown for a loop when one of them did have a bad day. Without much experience with mood swings, they didn't have the skills to weather the storm.

Wein can usually smooth things over.

Whenever Falanya's mood went south, it became Wein's responsibility to calm her. As the little sister, Falanya had no choice but to lay down her arms when her beloved brother admonished her.

This, unfortunately, wasn't an option for them right now.

Wein was absent from the palace—which was, coincidentally, the exact reason for her mood.

"It's not uncommon for Wein to leave for long stretches of time. Are you still having trouble adjusting?"

"No! That's not why I'm upset!"

So she *was* upset. Nanaki knew pointing that out wouldn't do him any favors.

"Then what's getting under your skin?"

"Isn't it obvious?!" Falanya snapped back, raising her voice. "Because he went off to a tropical island with Princess Tolcheila—of all people!"

It had all started in early autumn of the previous year. Two neighboring kingdoms—Natra and Soljest—had waged war on each other. Wein had formulated a strategy to topple the enemy army and capture King Gruyere. Natra had been granted partial rights to the port in Soljest, along with a hefty ransom and reparations.

"—Maritime trade has been lucrative for as long as it's been around."

Speaking in a low voice was Prince Wein, sitting in his office.

"But our climate means our access to the sea is frozen over for most of the year. Which makes it hard for us to benefit from maritime products," he continued.

His aide Ninym stood at attention by his side. She had the characteristic white hair and red eyes of the Flahm. Maintaining her silence, she listened to her sovereign.

"Meanwhile, the port of Soljest is usable all year round. We might be able to use this opportunity to open trade channels with other countries. That'll help explode our economy."

Wein's statement made total sense. The basic strategy of business was buying local products cheaply and selling them for high prices in faraway lands. Overseas trade meant raking in some serious profits.

"So..." Wein turned to Ninym. "What did other countries say about trading with us?"

"A resounding no."

"Nooooooo!" Wein landed a disappointed backflip. "That's just plain weird! No one?! Not a single one?! We've got Imperial goods! Isn't there a demand for those?! Come on! They know they want them! Please want them! Please!"

Even with the new trade route, the kingdom had no real industries, and none of their offerings had caught the attention of other countries. That was why Wein had been planning on buying up goods from the Empire to trade with nations in the West.

As Ninym pointed out, that was looking like a no-go.

"Why?!" Wein writhed in agony.

Ninym seemed defeated. "It has nothing to do with the merchandise. They're wary of you."

"Excuse you? They're wary of me? Why? All I did was lie that Imperial products were made in Natra, incite internal conflict in an already unstable nation, topple the leader of Levetia, and earn some huge winnings! What's wrong with that?!"

"If I were a politician, I would want nothing to do with you…"

He was an actual danger to society.

"Gaaaaah!" Wein clutched at his head, slamming it down. "This is bad news! We've already squandered our winnings to pay for our war efforts. As if that isn't bad enough, Levetia is keeping us at arm's length ever since we waged war on one of their Holy Elites!"

"If we don't do anything, we're going to keep bleeding money…"

"And listen to this! Gruyere was all like…"

"Hmm? You have no boats to use in our port? Ha-ha-ha. You know I'm on your side. I'll gladly let you use some…for a fee."

"Hmm? You have no sailors to employ on our boats in our port? Ha-ha-ha. You know I'm on your side. I'll gladly let you use some…for a fee."

"Hmm? You have no one to trade with, even though you have our sailors and boats? You want to borrow them after you've secured a trading partner?

"Ha-ha-ha. Hold fast, my prince. My sailors are busy men, and my ships tightly scheduled. You might miss a business opportunity if you *dawdle too long. I'm certain you'll find a business partner in no time... By the way, we should form a long-term contract that can't be terminated early. Might be cheaper that way."*

"—And I actually *agreed* to it! That pig knew I wouldn't find anyone to trade with!"

"He certainly got you good..."

"At this rate, we'll have nothing coming in, while our maintenance costs keep rising...! This isn't good...!"

It was critical that Wein find a trading partner as soon as possible.

"This would have been the perfect time to talk to government leaders—when they're staying put in their home countries...!"

"If we let this opportunity pass us by, it might be difficult to have a discussion even in a conference setting. After all, once the Gathering of the Chosen is rescheduled, they'll have their hands full."

The Gathering of the Chosen. Hosted once a year by the biggest religion of the Western continent, it was attended by Levetia's leaders, known as Holy Elites, and normally held in spring during the Festival of the Spirit. Many of the Holy Elites were political figures such as kings and dukes, and it wasn't uncommon for the event to be postponed if their schedules didn't line up.

That said, the Holy Elites couldn't exactly go into the new year without hosting the conference. There had never been one later than fall. Not that Wein could kick back just because it was still spring. If he didn't take this seriously, Levetia might settle on a date for the Gathering of the Chosen, which would postpone any discussions about trade.

"So they're scared of you and refuse to negotiate. What about trading with the East, where the Empire is?" Ninym asked.

"Yeah, except our best products are from the Empire."

Natra still didn't have any industries to speak of. If he sold its bad products to the Empire, he would make the kingdom pennies, and Natra would be the butt of its own joke. Likewise if he sold the Empire back its own products.

"Maybe we could sell stuff from Soljest to the Empire... No... I can totally see Gruyere using that chance to charge me up the wazoo...!"

That settled it. Their best option was to sell Imperial goods to Western nations. For better or for worse, Wein had become a household name...which meant it wouldn't be easy to form relations with other Western nations.

In short, it would take time to trade with other countries under current circumstances. And time was money. A negative feedback loop was ready to suck in Wein—one where he'd cry bloody murder whenever he bled more cash. He had to break the cycle somehow.

"Pardon me! Coming through!"

The door slammed open.

"Princess Tolcheila! What brings you here?" Wein asked, quickly correcting his posture.

Younger than Wein, Tolcheila was the crown princess of Soljest, which made her King Gruyere's daughter.

"I received word from my father that you may be in trouble, Prince Wein."

Ever since the war ended between Natra and Soljest, Tolcheila had been "studying abroad" in the kingdom. Basically, she was being held hostage.

That said, there was nothing hostage-like in her behavior. In fact, her brazen attitude was reminiscent of her father, King Gruyere.

"I heard tell you're anxious because you're left with no one to trade with, even though you've finally acquired the port. I have come to you with a proposal."

"A proposal?"

It went without saying that Tolcheila was an ally to neither Wein nor Natra. She and her homeland came first.

Both parties were aware of her priorities. Tolcheila must know Wein would spurn any proposal that served Soljest. If she was coming to him with an idea, it must have some benefit to them both.

"...All right, I'll hear you out. What do you have in mind?"

"Are you familiar with a kingdom called Patura, Prince?"

Wein nodded, screwing up his face a little. "An island nation at the farthest southern tip of the continent, right?"

"Indeed."

Patura. Also known as the Patura Archipelago. It was nestled in the sea, not too far from the southern tip of Varno—a cluster of small islands known for sustaining itself through international commerce.

"I imagine you know Soljest found great riches through trade. Though we're on opposite ends of Varno, we have connections in Patura since we're in the same industry."

"I see… So, in other words…"

Tolcheila nodded. "Patura is governed by the Zarif. The current head of the family, the sea guide—*Ladu*—is Alois Zarif. If I step in, he may grant you an audience. What say you? Will you try your luck in the Southern lands?"

Wein and Ninym exchanged looks.

They had considered trading with Patura. Its island values didn't align with those of the East or the West, and they had heard Levetia had almost no foothold there. As proof of this, the Flahm could apparently live normal lives there.

Wein had reason to believe they wouldn't care if he had bad blood with Levetia…but it didn't seem realistic to trade with them. After all, Patura was so far away. Though it was common practice to send local products to distant lands, their locations on opposite ends of the continent *felt* needlessly far.

The other reason it seemed impossible was the products themselves.

"Patura is on the opposite side of the continent from Natra—and the same distance away from the Empire. Is there even a need for us to ship them these goods?"

"Well," Tolcheila answered, "you ought to remember that the Empire has tried to conquer Patura as part of their imperialist agenda. The islands have managed to fend them off, but this has soured any chance of reconciliation. Meaning Imperial goods are not in wide circulation."

Emotionally distant from the Empire and culturally divorced from Levetia. If he didn't factor in distance, Wein could certainly see Patura as a viable option.

"If you're still unsure, I will allow Natra to sell our goods wholesale. I am your ally, Prince, so I can offer a more-than-fair price."

"......"

Tolcheila flashed him a mischievous grin. Wein's mind raced.

It certainly wasn't a bad deal. Tolcheila would act as his liaison until Wein could meet with a representative from Patura. After that, it would be up to the two kingdoms to seal the deal. It was better than wasting time running around with no solid plan.

King Gruyere must have calculated that Wein would come to this conclusion.

He's one sneaky pig.

The king must have known Wein wouldn't find a place to trade with so easily. And Wein wasn't the type to let an opportunity slide, especially with this new port. The princess would gauge the perfect moment to offer him a helping hand. In the end, he'd owe her for mediating the discussion, plus Soljest would now have a place to sell its wares.

As for making him sign a contract for the boats and seamen—well, that was just plain bullying.

The most infuriating part about this whole thing was that this was an offer too good to refuse.

Next time I see him, I'm turning Gruyere into a roast pig.
He'd reached his decision.

"Thank you for your offer, Princess Tolcheila… I would appreciate your facilitation."

"I figured. Let us send off a letter immediately."

In the note, Tolcheila introduced Wein to the representative of Patura, and Wein penned his own message. It wasn't long before they received a reply that essentially granted them an audience.

That was what landed Wein in the island nation of Patura.

Back to the present.

"Ugh! Ugh! Ugh! I've had enough of this brother of mine! He's so…! So…!"

Left behind in Natra, Falanya was throwing a fit with Nanaki as her audience.

"I wanted to go, too! But I'm stuck here, keeping house! How come Princess Tolcheila gets to go?! Ugh! No fair!"

Falanya flailed on the bed. This tantrum was a long one. She had a policy of not embarrassing herself in front of Nanaki, but that had totally gone out the window.

If she were a tyrant, Falanya would take out her rage on the officials. Since she was a good girl at heart, however, that would never happen. The only victim was the punched-in pillow in her bedroom.

Nanaki felt on edge whenever his master was in a mood. The officials were begging him to do something about it. He wasn't exactly the best at comforting people, but it was worth a try.

"Falanya."

"What?!"

"Tolcheila's body is just as childlike as yours, so I don't think it'll do anything for Wein."

His vision filled with pillow. Nanaki caught the projectile.

Falanya side-eyed him, moaning. "Hmph, I bet Wein is having a ball, under puffy white clouds and sailing over the deep blue sea! I'm going to give him a hard time as soon as he gets home!"

The window opened up to the sky.

Thinking of her brother under the same sun, she knew what she was going to do.

Meanwhile…

"—Well, then."

Blue ocean.

White clouds.

Sunbeams poured down.

Wein stared beyond *the iron bars of a jail cell.*

"Well, what am I gonna do?"

It was the third spring Wein had served as regent. The Kingdom of Natra could hardly be called powerless anymore.

This welcome change for its subjects was a source of tension for other countries.

This era, which was to be coined the Great War of Kings by future historians, was entering a new stage, one in which new trials and tribulations awaited the Kingdom of Natra.

Chapter 2 | From Surprise Incident to Surprise Meeting

A ship cruised across the ultramarine sea.

Its masts stretched up high, and the bottom of the ship swelled bulbously, giving it the shape of an acorn split in half. It was the size of a small hill. Only trees as tall as the heavens could ever produce an acorn of this size.

This type of vessel was known as a "carrack," primarily serving as a trade ship that voyaged across oceans. It wasn't propelled forward by humans rowing oars, but by three thick, white sails that hung on masts to catch the wind.

This time, the boat wasn't making a shipment. It was transporting the representative of Natra—Wein—to the Patura Archipelago.

"Gweh…"

At the moment, the representative in question was slumped listlessly on the couch of his cabin. Seasick.

"You're like this every time you're at sea. You always feel better whenever we reach the port and touch land… Seems like you and boats just don't mesh, Wein."

Ninym watched over him worriedly from a chair next to him. She was feeling fine.

"I was surprised myself… It's not just the rocking of the boat… I mean, the weather…"

"Yeah. It's warm for early spring."

Patura was on the far southern tip of the mainland. Obviously, its weather was going to be different from Natra's. Wein was lightly dressed, but his body was having trouble adjusting to the extreme change in temperature, especially since a brutal winter had just ended in the North.

Not that he was weak. Ninym was just special. She had the aptitude to navigate these unfamiliar circumstances—from the boat ride to the extreme weather—with just a simple outfit change.

"We should arrive on the Patura Archipelago sometime today. Try to hang on until then."

"Uh-huh… I'll try."

Ninym wasn't being totally honest. She said it mostly to console him. Upon departing from the port in Soljest, the ship had made a western circuit, stopping at a few ports for supplies, and it was now in the final stretch. Patura was just within its reach.

If all went well, the ship would arrive at some point during the day. Problem was, it was impossible to predict the whims of the sea. If the ship got caught in a storm, a safe arrival wasn't guaranteed for anyone.

"Well, you know where I'll be," Wein muttered. "Let me know when you see Patura…"

"Understood. I'll be outside."

She was worried about him, but it wasn't like his seasickness would get any better with her hovering over him.

"Here's hoping our return trip will be on land…" Wein groaned from behind as she slipped out of the cabin.

"—Omph."

The door was only one step away from the deck of the ship. Ninym drank in the briny air and strong rays. She scraped back her flyaway hairs with her hand, heading toward the ship's bow.

"Oh, if it isn't Ninym."

The voice belonged to Tolcheila. She must have been staring out over the ocean with her attendants. The rocking of the boat didn't trouble her. The princess approached Ninym with practiced, confident steps.

"How fares the prince?"

"Better, but he'll need to rest."

A white lie. Ninym needed to save face for her liege's sake.

"Hmm. It's probably best that we arrive in Patura quickly, then. It's unfortunate that he cannot enjoy this view." Tolcheila looked out over the ocean and shook her head in disappointment.

Ninym looked at her. *Like father like daughter*, she thought. *She's such a go-getter.*

Though Tolcheila was the one to volunteer to act as intermediary, the crown princess *was* accompanying them to the other end of the continent. This had triggered Falanya's rotten mood, but Ninym had never expected a royal to be so accommodating.

She reminds me of Lowa.

Lowellmina, Ninym's good friend and the Imperial Princess of the Earthworld Empire. During their school days, Lowa had never been predicable. Ninym had seen her as a wild card.

"—*Achoo!*"

"Feeling sick, Princess Lowellmina?"

"I'm fine, Fyshe. I think someone's talking behind my back. I'm allergic to gossip, you know."

"...Are you certain it's not because of your stomach-exposing outfit?"

"Do you hear yourself? Listen, Fyshe. A good outfit can make or break your day. You can't get cold if you're in a good mood. Besides, it's already spring! I overcame winter with nothing but this attitude, so this is a walk in the park!"

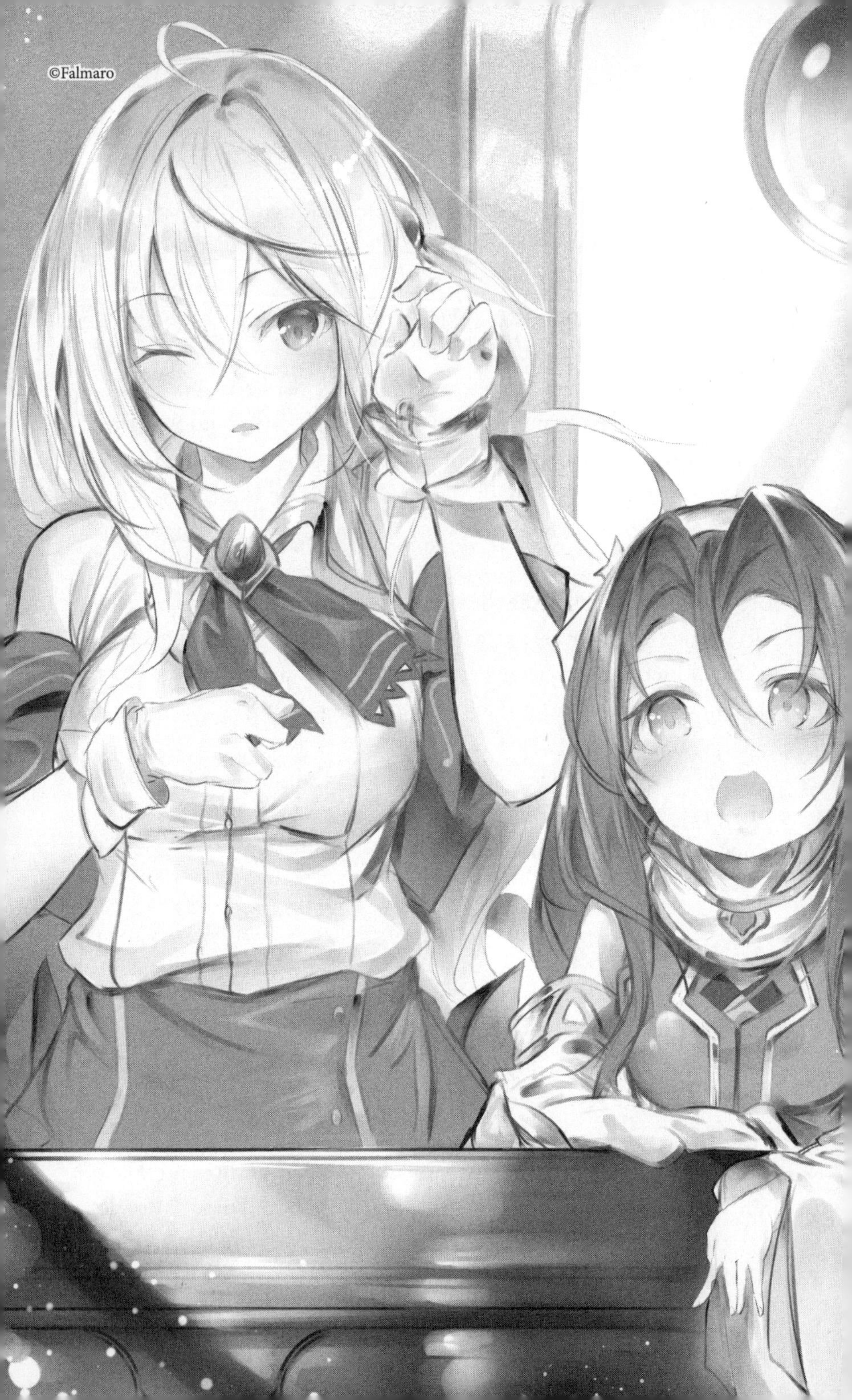
©Falmaro

"Is that so?"

"It is!" Lowellmina insisted.

Obviously, her accompanying us helps out Natra.

Everything came down to human connection. That was why Wein was making the visit in person, since they couldn't settle anything via mail. Tolcheila acting as their liaison would only make the deal easier.

But it almost seems like she's only here because she wants to be out at sea...

Ninym had initially assumed Tolcheila was trying to make them forever indebted to her, but watching the little princess scurry around on the ship had made the aide think otherwise.

Well, if she has no problem talking to me, she's already a little strange.

Ninym was a Flahm, oppressed in the Western nations for her white hair and red eyes, as dictated by Levetian doctrine. Treated as slaves, her people were stripped of human rights.

King Gruyere had provided the crew and Tolcheila's attendants, which meant they weren't about to disrespect foreign representatives, even if Ninym exposed her natural features. That said, she could feel the awkwardness in their every move. She knew it wasn't her imagination.

Like King Gruyere, however, Tolcheila didn't show the slightest bit of prejudice. Curious about this, Ninym had once indirectly asked why.

"*I am the master of myself. Not my father, not my spouse, not even God may command me. Why must I abide by something on a piece of paper? The people may have to cater to me, but I would never cater to people.*"

It was almost narcissistic, though strangely not in a bad way. Far from it, in fact. Ninym embraced Tolcheila for who she was and recognized the princess had a high opinion of her.

This informality reminds me of Lowa...

* * *

"Achoo-achoo!"

"Your Highness…"

"I-I'm fine! This is because of all the gossip! So maybe I get chilly on occasion. It would be foolish—all for nothing—if I give in now. Besides, there's no going back. And I'm definitely not cold…!"

"Shall I clear away this warm mead?"

"Bullying is a bad look for you, Fyshe…!"

I wonder what she's doing right about now?

Lowa was gulping down mead. Not that Ninym had any way of knowing that.

"—Land ho!" the lookout boy shouted from the platform halfway up the mainmast.

"It seems we've finally arrived," Ninym noted.

Tolcheila shook her head. "Not yet. This is only the entrance to the Patura Archipelago."

"The entrance?"

"Right. There's a cluster of bigger and smaller islands. Each one is ruled by a different clan and people of influence, but the stronghold of the Zarif is the island in the very center. It's right beyond the island we see."

"I see. Hence calling it the entrance."

"Indeed. We'll be there in no time… Mm?" Tolcheila was looking at someone behind Ninym. Turning around to follow her gaze, Ninym saw Wein had left his cabin.

"Your Highness." Ninym hurried over to Wein.

His complexion was dull, and he staggered forward.

"Is it all right for you to be up?"

"I'm managing," Wein assured her. "Anyway, I heard we can see the island?"

"Yes. But only the one that acts as the door to Patura. Our destination is farther ahead."

"Oh..." Wein leaned over the ship's rail, looking deflated.

"Hee-hee. To think the prince's sprits have been dashed by a simple boat ride."

Wein tried to straighten his posture as Tolcheila approached, but he was too slow.

"Please pardon my unsightly appearance, Princess Tolcheila."

"Think nothing of it. Aging and illness are a natural part of life. In fact, I'm delighted to see this side of you, Prince."

Her chuckle brought a strained smile to Wein's face.

"Seems you're as cheerful as ever, Princess... Even with no seasickness, I thought anyone would find this long journey exhausting."

"I'm used to setting sail. That said, this is only my second visit to Patura. After all, it's hard to depart for a land as far as this one at a moment's notice."

The boat sailed toward the island. It continued forward, tracing the island's outline into Patura's inner ocean.

"...Strange," Tolcheila murmured under her breath.

"What's the matter?" Wein asked.

"I don't see signs of any other ships. Last time, I passed many of them around here."

"Now that you mention it, it seems strange that there aren't many ships near an island trading post— Ah."

Wein looked out. It was as if they'd been heard. A single ship slipped into view on the western side of the island. It was a carrack just like theirs.

Spoke too soon, Wein thought.

The ship raised several emblemed flags up the masts. The crew began to stir.

"Hey, that flag is ordering us to stop."

"Who does the ship belong to? The Zarif?"

"I've never seen that emblem before."

"Put up our signal flag. We'll tell them we're carrying a delegation."

The crew snapped into action. One of them turned and spoke to Tolcheila.

"Pardon me, Lady Tolcheila. Something about their ship seems strange. They may be pirates."

"Pirates, eh? Don't the Zarif control these waters?"

"Yes, that should be the case. However..." The crew member trailed off.

A lookout called down to them. "The vessel is of unknown origin, and it's speeding toward us!"

"They're not responding to our flag signal? Damn! I knew it. Pirates!"

"All hands to your stations! We'll go around to the east to make our escape!" shouted one of the crew.

Maritime battles meant striking the enemy ship with the naval ram attached to the fore or climbing over grappling hooks onto a nearby boat to engage in hand-to-hand combat. On their ship built for commercial trade, however, there was no naval ram, and the crew had no real battle experience. Meaning that if these were indeed pirates, there was no chance of winning a fight.

Tolcheila seemed racked with nerves, questioning the ship's crew. "Will we be able to get away?"

"...It seems we're moving at the same speed. The wind is on our side, so I predict we will be able to escape. Even if we can't shake them completely, we will eventually be saved by a guard ship as long as we maintain this distance."

Their ship changed direction and skirted the eastern side of the island. The pirate-like ship pursued them, but the distance gradually widened.

"Hmm. Will this be enough?" Tolcheila asked the seaman.

"Most likely. Just to be safe, I would like everyone to retreat inside. It will be safer there and put our crew's mind at ease."

It was the nicest way to let them know they were in the way. Since the guests didn't know the first thing about running a ship, this decision was instant.

Wein was going obediently inside when—

"Starboard! Another unknown ship detected!" the lookout shrieked.

They all turned to the right, the direction of the island. Another vessel appeared from the shadows as if to block their path.

"Steer to port side!"

"—We won't make it in time! We're going to crash!"

A collision violently rocked the ship—an impact bigger than any wave. The vessel veered forcefully to the left.

"—Ah."

Who had produced that small shriek?

Stomach churning, Wein gripped the side of the boat. Tolcheila was instantly surrounded by crew and attendants.

They saw Ninym's body thrown toward the sea.

"Ninym!" Wein didn't hesitate for a second. He reached out, gripping her and spinning around until they switched places.

There was nothing supporting him now.

"Wein!" Ninym shrieked as he plunged into the ocean.

Everything changed in an instant. No air. His nose and ears filled with seawater.

He struggled to the surface, where he witnessed Ninym about to leap off the boat to rescue him.

"STAY BACK!" Wein shouted.

Ninym froze.

Their ship had veered away from the other vessel and started to move again.

From a distance, he could see Ninym and Tolcheila screaming at the crew to do something—*anything*—but the ship did not stop. As if to escape the clutches of the enemy, it raced across the ocean at top speed.

Wein was left to fend for himself...

"—*Phew.*"

He let out a little sigh of relief—not one of despair or worry.

The ship and crew were on loan from King Gruyere. Therefore, the crew prioritized Princess Tolcheila over Wein. They didn't have time to collect idiots going overboard, especially with pirates on their tail. Even if said idiots were foreign royalty or their attendants.

The island is right there. It won't be that hard to swim to shore. The real problem is...

Tasting the seawater in his mouth, Wein looked around him and spotted the original pirate ship fast approaching. The vessel pulled right up next to Wein, furled its sails, and came to a halt. A rope ladder came crashing down before him.

...Guess I've got no choice but to hop on.

It wasn't like he could outswim a ship.

Plus, he wouldn't stand a chance if they got him with spears or harpoons. And even if he did reach the island before they killed him, it could belong to his attackers.

Wein clutched the rope ladder and made his way aboard.

Blade tips were waiting for him when he got there.

"Well, yeah, I guess I expected this." Wein raised his hands in front of the sword-wielding crew. "I'm not going to resist, so I'd like you to lower your weapons."

He quickly took note of each member.

Full sets of matching armor on all of them. Same thing with their weapons. Anyone would think this was a warship, but these aren't the Zarif…

The apparent captain of the ship stepped forward.

"Someone has some guts, eh? Looks like you're not just some manservant. You'll sell high." He dragged the tip of his blade across Wein's throat. "Boy, do you know where that ship came from and where it's going?"

"……" Wein suddenly pieced together what the man was after.

Even if he didn't know whom the ship belonged to, his goal had to be one thing—money.

"From Soljest," Wein said. "It's looking to buy up goods from Patura."

A perfectly believable answer of half-truths. If these people's objective was money, it was better to make them think he was from a normal merchant ship rather than reveal the vessel was carrying foreign dignitaries.

"Soljest, huh… Must have been a long journey to make it down from the north of nowhere."

"Can you cut me some slack, then? Between you and me, I was just attacked by pirates and flung into the ocean."

"Hmph. Don't get too cocky, boy. We were just approaching the ship to conduct an inspection, but there seems to be a bit of a misunderstanding, since they turned tail on us."

"'Inspection'…? What, is there a war going on or something?"

"I have no obligation to tell you. Just pray you fetch us a good price… Lock this guy away in the ship's hold!"

Wein's arms were bound behind him with rope before he was

tossed into the hold. Sooner than he could even struggle to his feet, the ship lurched forward.

Can't say I was expecting this.

Where was the ship headed? What was going on in Patura? What would happen to him?

The ship cruised over the sea, carrying the unknowing prince.

The ship must have anchored in a military port.

Lining the harbor were rows of identical ships. A large fortress loomed over them. One glance was enough to tell anyone that this heavily patrolled structure was important.

Wein was led inside the fortress by the ship's crew. It seemed ancient, with traces of repairs patching up the walls. The building had to be several decades old, but it had never been vacant. In fact, Wein could tell the facility had been in use since its construction.

They arrived at the jail.

"This one's yours. Go on. Get inside."

Wein had never seen anything so unsanitary in his life, but he obliged.

"We'll come back to question you later. Don't cause any trouble."

With that, the ship's crew slammed the door shut, locking him in, and left.

When Wein couldn't hear their footsteps anymore, he let out a little sigh.

"Well, what am I gonna do?"

Lucky for him, they had untied his hands. Wein looked around the cell, rooting through it for something useful. Sure enough, he found nothing.

Well, it is *a jail cell.*

Wein reached out to touch the bars covering his window. It didn't seem like he'd be able to remove them on his own. Beyond the window, the ocean and sky seemed to stretch out forever. This fortress seemed to be built on a steep cliff, so even if he somehow managed to escape, he'd tumble headfirst right off the edge.

Obviously, the other bars on the door didn't seem like they would budge. He didn't know how to pick locks with a wire. Not that he had any wires on him to begin with.

He tried to give the bars a good jiggle, unwilling to give up.

"—Is someone there?" someone called out from the cell next to him.

It was a man's voice. Wein couldn't see his face since there was a stone wall between them, but he sounded terribly frail and exhausted.

Wein didn't hesitate to reply. "Yeah. I'm your new prison neighbor."

He didn't know what this guy's deal was, but he desperately needed information.

"I got caught on my ship when I came to do some merchant business," the prince said. "I planned to make landfall sometime today, but I never thought these would be my accommodations."

"I'm sorry to hear that… Where did you come from?"

"Soljest."

"…Then I bet you were surprised. The truth is, Patura is dealing with an issue at the moment."

"Some dignitary waving a banner of rebellion?"

Wein could almost feel his neighbor's surprise through the wall.

"Did you already hear the rumors?"

"Just a guess based on the information I've gleaned so far. From your reaction, I'm guessing I'm right."

His captors had been engaged in pirate activity in Zarif-controlled waters, approaching ships from unknown origins as part of an "investigation."

Their equipment was just too good for pirates. Even this facility seemed too fancy. He'd pieced it all together and begun to see the hazy outline of an answer.

Someone had successfully attacked the Zarif and taken over Patura, facility and all.

"...You're right. This all started when the Zarif's *Ladu*, Alois Zarif, was assassinated by pirates."

"*Urp.*" Wein gulped.

"Something the matter?"

"...Nothing."

Alois Zarif. The representative Wein was supposed to meet. He'd prepared himself for this news when he'd heard the domain was in the hands of someone else, but hearing it confirmed made Wein groan.

"Were the pirates that strong?"

"That and Patura has maelstroms known as Dragon Storms around this time of year. I heard the pirates attacked during one of those."

"Dragon Storms, huh...?"

They were a natural phenomenon impossible in Natra. They must have been because of Patura's tropical climate.

"When Patura was in shambles from the loss of its *Ladu*, a certain man led a fleet of ships to wage an attack against us. They were swift, and Patura had no one to take command, so the islands were under their control in an instant."

"He must have been corroborating with the pirates from the very start. Who was this guy?"

"...Legul Zarif. Alois's eldest son. A natural genius who knows the sea like the back of his hand. The man once next in line to be the *Ladu*. He was banished from Patura for terrorizing the citizens."

"I see…"

Wein had thought the whole thing was awfully clever, so it made sense if a local had been the one to spearhead everything.

"He was the original successor. Legul's fleet is expanding its domain as the island leaders fail to work together to subjugate him, even now. With everything else going on, I hear unsavory characters are attacking passing ships, seizing cargo, and taking people hostage for ransom. I take it that's what happened to you."

"Bingo…" Wein moaned.

Trouble just seemed to follow him around. His negotiating partner was dead, and Wein had gotten captured, caught up in some random war.

"I'm terribly sorry…" said the man through the wall.

Wein cocked his head to the side. "Hey. This is your second time apologizing. You haven't done anything wrong…right?"

The root of the problem was this Legul Zarif. He was the one who should be taking responsibility. The only other person who could apologize would have been his father, Alois Zarif.

The prisoner wouldn't let it go. "No, I should be apologizing. After all, I—"

"Hey! What're you yammering on about?!"

Soldiers stepped into the corridor. They stopped in front of Wein's cell, unlocking his door, and began barking orders at him.

"Get out! We got some questions for you!"

"Okay, okay. No need to raise your voice." Wein exited the cell without objection.

He glanced farther down the jail and caught sight of a man leaning against the iron bars.

The haggard man looked at Wein and silently mouthed, *"Be careful."*

Wein was hauled off to an interrogation room.

Tools for "questioning" were straightened on the table. The smell of blood soaked the walls and floor, enough to paralyze the weak of heart.

The chief interrogator awaiting him spoke in a cavalier tone. "I will inform you right now that I will not negotiate with you in any capacity."

The man glared at Wein.

"Your crimes are serious—slighting our flags asking you to stop for the inspection, damaging our ships, fleeing from the scene. You will not be allowed to leave here alive if the price for your crimes remains unpaid."

The heaviness of his voice warned this wasn't an idle threat.

However, Wein remained undaunted, naturally. In fact, to him, this information held a bit of good news.

In other words, the others haven't been caught.

Wein was relieved for two reasons.

First, the man's words meant everyone else had safely escaped. Second, they meant Wein had allies on the outside who could help him get out of here.

"Hey! Are you listening?!" The interrogator slammed his fist against the table, trying to intimidate him.

"Of course I'm listening. So how much will it take to release me?"

"Hmm? Confident, are we? ...Let's see how long that smug look of yours lasts. Listen closely. Your ransom is five thousand gold coins!"

The soldiers huddled around the interrogator seemed surprised. This was only reasonable; ransom was usually set at a few gold coins. Maybe a dozen for really important people. Even figuring in the ship repairs, five thousand coins was ridiculous.

A cocky brat, huh? the interrogator thought. *I'll have him begging for mercy.*

An evil look spread across his face. Everyone around him could tell this monetary amount was something he had arbitrarily come up with himself.

"...Hey," Wein said.

"You can't talk yourself out of this one. We already agreed on those terms. I'll add another hundred coins every time you run your little mouth. Still have something to say?"

"Make it *two hundred thousand*."

Only Wein knew what that meant.

It wasn't as if they didn't understand him. They just thought they'd heard him wrong.

There was no stopping Wein. "Five thousand is too little. If you need me to pay, I'll make it two hundred thousand gold coins."

There was no mistaking it this time. After a beat, the interrogator pounded his fist on the desk.

"What the hell are you talking about?! Two hundred thousand?! Are you screwing with me?!"

"Not at all. I'm completely serious." Wein shrugged. "I'm the treasurer of Lontra and Co. in Soljest. It has a mountain of coins that don't move without my orders. Two hundred thousand coins will be no problem. I'll pay you in full."

What the hell is with this guy? I have no clue what he's talking about.

For some reason, the interrogator and soldiers found themselves hanging on Wein's every word.

"As for my ship...it likely escaped to the Salendina Company in

Patura. After all, they're one of Lontra's major business partners. Things should move quickly if you contact them."

"B-but...if that's true... Oh right! What's your objective?! If you've got that much money, why wouldn't you just cough up the five thousand?! What's the point in making things harder for yourself?!"

"I love money, but I love my life more. If my guys abandoned me, that tells me my life isn't worth very much to them. But I'm still alive. They misjudged me. You know, merchants always make the appropriate people suffer appropriate damages. Think of it as a form of revenge."

There was neither authority nor servility in his voice. Everyone sensed he was merely speaking the truth.

Wein questioned them with a smile.

"So what will you do? Two hundred thousand gold coins is enough to change the lives of everyone here. Of course, if you want to keep up your modest ways of living, you're free to ask for five thousand. There's no harm in that, though I can't imagine why you would ever refuse my proposal."

All present knew there was no downside to this deal. It was just a matter of raising the ransom from five thousand to two hundred thousand. They'd make 195,000 extra coins—free of charge.

But they were still conflicted. It was just too sudden, too ridiculous, too tempting.

Wein was ready to mentally corner them and pounce.

"One hundred and ninety thousand."

The soldiers jumped in their skins.

"You guys are impossible. No good at all. If you're going to dither about a deal this simple, I have no choice but to lower the ransom. If you're still not sure, I'll lower it until you accept."

"What?! W-wait!"

Wein had gained total control of the situation, but he was the only one who realized this.

"No waiting. Time is money. If you squander time deciding, you lose precious gold. Isn't that obvious? So? What will you do? One hundred and eighty thousand—and less by the second."

"O-okay! We'll contact Salendina! That's all we have to do, right?!"

Wein clapped. "Excellent! Bring a bed to my cell before that. Oh, and a desk and chair. I'll need some quality wine. Plus—"

"D-don't be ridiculous! As if we'd agree to that!"

"Would you leave a two-hundred-thousand-coin wine outside? Set it down in a corner of a jail cell? You wouldn't, would you? Keeping valuables in mint condition takes a certain level of labor. If you can't hand me over in perfect health, my value will diminish. Obviously."

"B-but you're our prisoner."

"One hundred and seventy thousand."

The men shuddered at the new ransom amount.

Wein flashed them an arrogant smile. "So what will you do? I should mention there's no room to negotiate."

"How did we even get here…?"

"Hell if I know. Just hurry up and prepare the bed…!"

Badgered by Wein, the soldiers hauled a bed, a desk, a chair, and various other furnishings into the cell. By the time they realized it would have been easier to move him into a guest room in the fortress, the bare stone cell had become outfitted with enough to accommodate anyone.

"Well, I suppose this is a bit better."

Wein lounged on the bed with a wine bottle in one hand.

The jail cell wasn't all that bad for Wein, who'd marched for long periods and slept outside before. But he was in desperate need of a stationary bed after being jostled by the ship during the journey here.

"...Amazing."

He heard a voice from the cell next to him.

"I can't imagine how you managed to pull that off."

The man must have been watching through the iron bars as everything was jammed into Wein's cell. He sounded impressed, though his comment was mixed with a dry chuckle.

"You'd be surprised how far a conversation takes you. Care for some wine?"

"No, thank you. Those are your spoils. I do not deserve your kindness," the man said firmly yet politely. "There is one thing I must ask."

He took a deep breath.

"Aren't you Prince Wein?"

"'Prince Wein'?"

Wein sounded like he suddenly couldn't remember his own name.

"I'm afraid you've got the wrong man. My name is Glen," Wein said quickly, borrowing the name of a good friend.

His mind raced furiously.

The soldiers regarded Wein as a merchant who would give them money. What would happen if they found out he was a high-profile foreigner?

It was unrealistically optimistic to think they'd apologize for their actions and escort him to a royal suite. After all, these guys had been planning to pillage his vessel as part of their "investigation." If

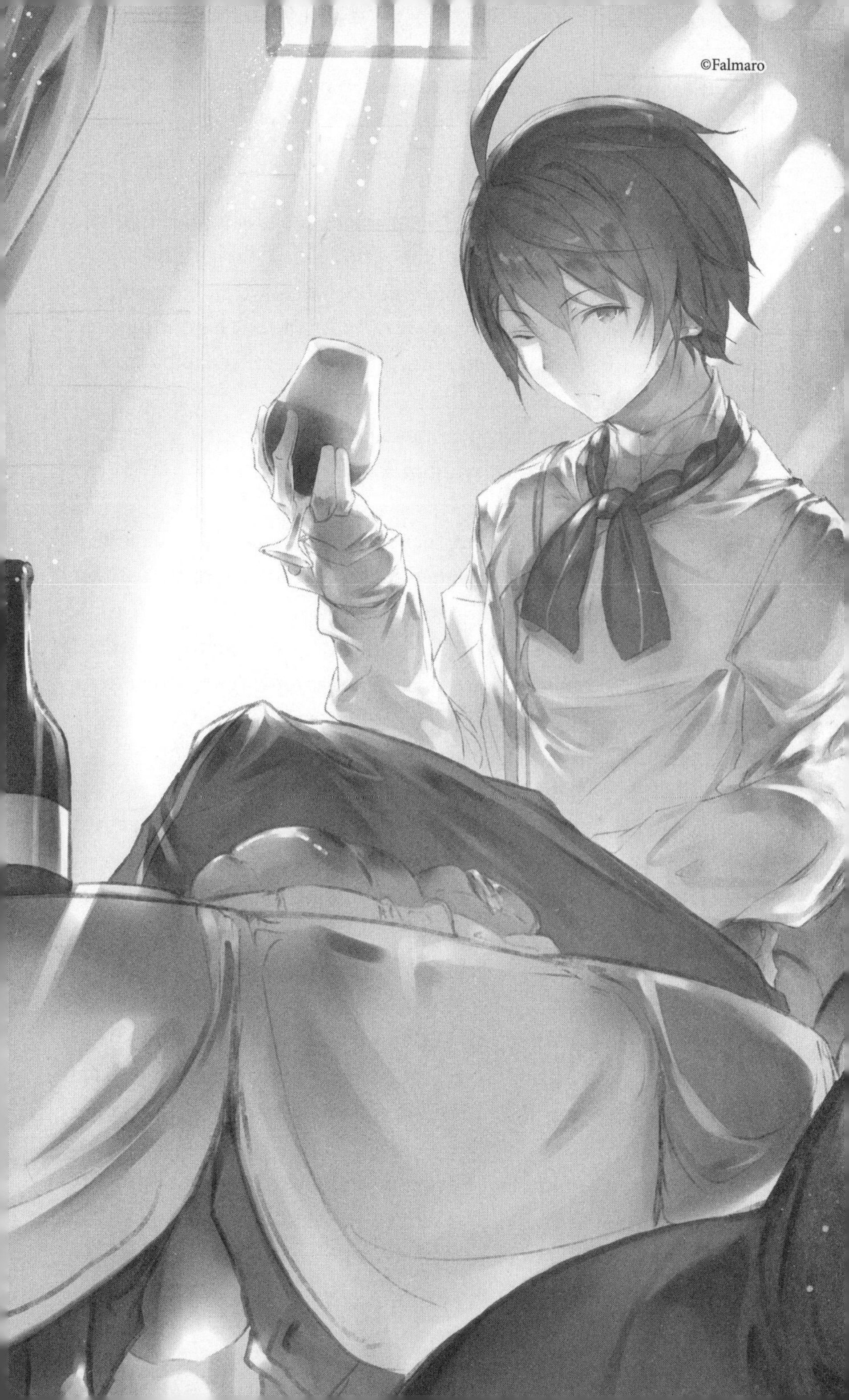
©Falmaro

they found out they'd attacked a ship carrying a foreign delegation, there was a good chance they'd kill Wein to bury their crimes.

I can't let anyone in this fortress know my identity.

It was up to him to crush any possibility of that happening. He would have to lie to this man and possibly even silence him if it came down to it.

"I see… I was mistaken. My apologies."

The man backed down without a fight—whether he could read Wein's mind or not.

The prince could have cut their conversation there, but he was curious to know why the man had suspected who he was in the first place.

"Hmm, Prince Wein, huh? The young hero leading the Kingdom of Natra? A diplomat skilled with pen and sword? A specimen more handsome than humanly imaginable?"

"I haven't heard a single thing about his looks."

"……"

They were only silent for a moment. Wein pulled himself together.

"So why did you mistake me for Prince Wein?"

"The first thing that caught my attention was your intonation. It speaks of a quality education. Second, you arrived right as the vessel carrying Prince Wein's delegation was scheduled to arrive in Patura."

Wein's eyes instantly grew sharp.

"I see… Impressive that you mistook me for the prince just from my way of speaking. And how did you know when a foreign envoy would be arriving?"

"It's my duty to know… Come to think of it, I failed to introduce myself before."

The man seemed to command the jail.

"The name's Felite Zarif. I'm the son of the previous *Ladu*, Alois Zarif, and the younger brother of Legul Zarif."

"——" Surprise colored Wein's expression.

The son of Alois, Felite. Wein had heard of him but had never expected him to be right here.

What's going on——?

Upon Alois's death, Felite should have taken his position as the next *Ladu*—and been killed by his older brother, Legul, as soon as the rebellion started.

Except he was alive now, in prison.

Is he lying about being Felite? But he has no reason to lie to me.

The gears in Wein's mind turned, trying to churn out questions that would help him get to the bottom of things. As if to interrupt his thought process, Wein could hear the pattering of feet coming down the corridor toward them.

There was no choice but to cut the conversation short. Wein leaned against the cell wall.

Coming into the corridor were soldiers led by a single man. Based on his clothes and the soldiers' behavior, he had to be someone very important.

Wein pegged him for the fortress's commanding officer. The man brushed past him, casting a fleeting glance his way. His feet stopped in front of the cell next to Wein.

"Hmph. Looks like you still have some life in you, Felite."

"Yes… Thanks to this comfortable cell, Brother."

Brother.

So, this was Legul, the rebel. And the man in the next cell over was Felite. Wein strained his ears to hear their conversation.

"How long do you plan on keeping this up? You think help will actually come for you?"

"……"

"I've already gained full control of the central island. The opposition was uncoordinated. Crushing them was easier than taking candy from a newborn babe. Get it through your head, Felite. Your fate was sealed long ago."

The man—Legul—sneered at his brother.

"I bet you're thinking about the future of the islanders, aren't you? You've always been meaninglessly altruistic. If you really feel that way, you should understand that the fastest way to end this rebellion is to make every citizen of Patura kneel before me."

Legul seemed to gain strength with each word.

"If you care about the future of these islands, there is only one thing you can do. Tell me where the Rainbow Crown is. Spit it out."

The Rainbow Crown. Wein flinched.

The name had come up while he was researching Patura. Its true form was—

"Brother…I have looked up to you since we were kids," Felite said suddenly. "No one could match you as a seaman. I, an ordinary layman, always admired you. I was certain you would be the next *Ladu*."

"Oh, so you've come around." Legul pressed him to continue.

"However," Felite said. "Do you honestly think I would hand over the islands to our parents' murderer? Leave this place, Legul Zarif! Glory will never come to someone who chases the edges of a rainbow without thinking about the rest of us!"

Metal clanged. Legul had struck the iron bars.

"You think you can tell me what to do? You—the second-choice *Ladu*?" Legul's voice was thick with unbridled rage. "Don't get carried away, Brother. Have you forgotten that my mercy is the only reason you're still clinging to your pathetic life?"

"You're the one who's forgotten the unforgettable. I imagine you'll never remember it... I hate to see you this way, Brother."

"...It seems I'll have to remind you of your place." Legul radiated the primal urge to kill. "Take him to the interrogation room. Use whatever methods you want. Make him tell you where the Rainbow Crown is."

"U-understood!"

"Rejoice, Felite. Once you confess, I will snap your neck myself... I'm going back up. Tell me as soon as he says anything."

His business finished, Legul turned on his heel. He passed by Wein's cell again—and stopped.

"...Hey, who's this kid?"

"Ah, a crew member that was thrown overboard from a suspicious ship we spotted the other day. We're keeping him captive until we find out more..."

"And you're treating him like this?"

Wein was not living the life of a normal prisoner—equipped with a fancy bed and desk.

"Um, well, uh..."

How could the soldier possibly explain?

It was Wein who came to his rescue.

"Ah, I'm very sorry. I have a weak constitution, and I had them prepare more than I should have been given."

"Th-that's right. It would spell trouble if something happened before we finished our investigation, so..."

Legul looked at Wein's complexion and snorted. "Hmph. You're telling me this man is frail? If you're trying to make a quick buck, you should at least hide it from me. If you dare get on my nerves, I'll make sure you sink in the sea—ship and all."

"Y-yes, sir!" The solider nodded over and over.

Legul fixed Wein with one final side-eyed glare before leaving the room. The remaining soldiers shuffled out, dragging Felite to the interrogation room.

Now all alone, Wein leaned against the stone wall, whispering to himself:

"Well, what am I gonna do?"

A handful of days had passed since Wein had been brought to this place.

In that time, he'd achieved nothing.

Ever since the interaction with Legul, the soldiers on patrol had started to act like they were being watched, snubbing Wein and rejecting his attempts to establish a conversation.

As for Felite, he'd been battered in the interrogation room, leaving him too exhausted to talk.

At this rate, he won't last much longer, Wein assessed.

Obviously, he didn't want his information bank to die. Wein had tried to offer him food through the iron bars, but Felite would refuse each time, saying very little. Even the prince thought it was a lost cause.

If only he felt like there was some chance of rescue...

Wein looked through the bars of his cell window. He had wrapped a white cloth around one of the bars, which flapped outside like a tail. Wein had fashioned it from a ripped corner of his bedsheet.

He could see gray clouds in the distant sky. The whistling wind carried the voices of the patrol guards outside.

"Wind is really picking up," one of them noted.

"It's unavoidable this time of year, but this is something else. Storm might be brewing."

"I sure hope we don't capsize while on patrol."

He listened to the guards in the distance as he lay on his bed.

...I hope they make it in time.

Wein shut his eyes, lying there silently.

Things began to change once the sun went down.

Wein thought he heard something: muffled voices coming from the guards' usual spot. As he jumped up from the bed, someone came sprinting down the dimly lit corridor.

"Wein…!"

It was Ninym. She raced toward him, almost tripping over herself, and he held out his hands through the iron bars. Ninym drew near enough to stroke his face.

"I'm so glad you're okay…!"

"Yeah, somehow. I'm relieved to see you got away."

"Forget about me! We have to get you out of there…!"

It took her several tries to get the key in the lock—hands fumbling from relief or panic. When Ninym finally opened the cell door, she flung herself into Wein's arms.

"Are you okay?! Did they hurt you while you were captured?! Is there anything unusual about your body?!"

"I'm okay, really."

Ninym blurted out a stream of questions as she checked over Wein's entire body, patting him down. Wein stroked her back, drawing her closer.

"Why did you have to be so reckless and jump into the ocean for me…?!"

"I thought it'd be better than you getting captured."

"You shouldn't be thinking about me! You didn't have to do that!"

"Don't be this way. That's what was the best choice for me."

Ninym pounded on his chest. He let this go on for some time.

"Your Highness, Lady Ninym," ventured a nervous voice from behind her.

Ninym quickly unwound herself from Wein's arms.

"Hurry. There isn't much time."

Ninym wasn't the only one who had sneaked in. Two soldiers from Natra had joined her in this rescue mission.

"R-right. —Your Highness, we've prepared a boat for your rescue. We must escape before we're found."

Ninym cleared her throat, marking her switch from normal girl to loyal servant. Wein nodded and exited the cell, but he stopped right before the one next to him.

"Your Highness…?"

"Ninym, open this cell."

"Y-yes." Ninym obliged, though she seemed hesitant, and immediately noticed the limp human form collapsed in the cell. She rushed over to take his pulse.

"How is he?"

"…He's alive, but severely weakened. He'll be in trouble if we leave him here. Who is this man?"

"Patura's trump card." Wein smiled. "Well, he has the potential to be."

"You want to take him with us?"

"Can we?"

"As long as he's the only one."

Ninym gave orders to one of the soldiers to carry the man out. The group would consist of one person in need of protection, one extra load, and two people to clear a path. But that shouldn't pose any problems.

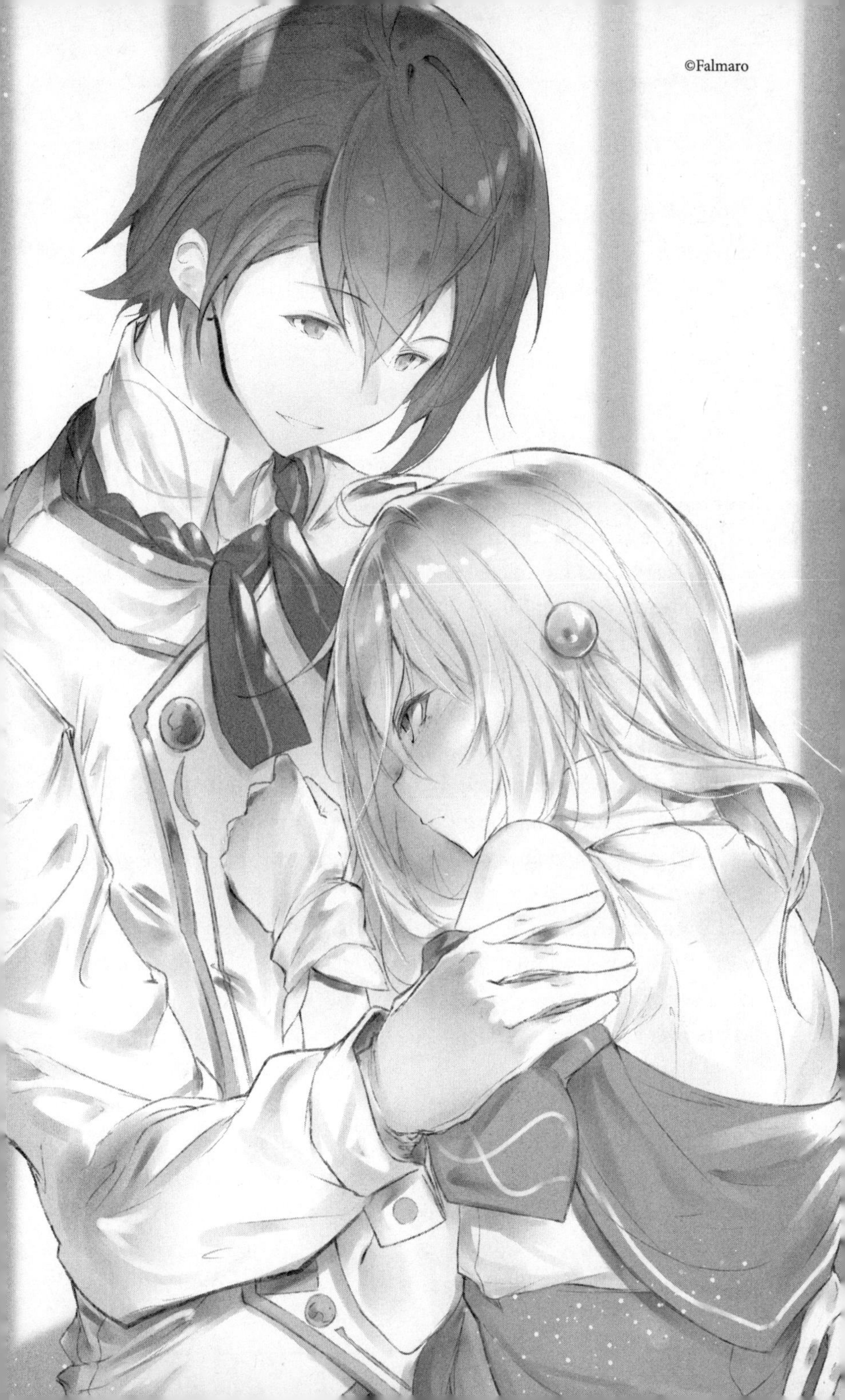

"Well, then, Your Highness. We must leave as quickly and quietly as possible."

With Ninym leading the way, they continued soundlessly down the hallway.

In the commander's room, Legul stared outside, stewing in his bad mood.

His plan was proceeding almost exactly as intended. After being exiled, Legul had connected with foreign dignitaries and increased his influence, waiting for an opportune moment. When his chance came, he disguised himself as a pirate and murdered his father, who had set out to subjugate him, under cover of a storm. After that, he raided central Patura and made it his own. Legul declared himself the rightful heir, subduing opposing islands with force—

Everything was going well. It was just as he'd planned.

Aside from knowing the location of the Rainbow Crown.

...Without the hidden treasure, I will never completely dominate these waters...!

He knew Felite had acted as bait so his subordinates could escape with the Rainbow Crown. Any sort of clue would help, but it seemed his rival had taken proper precautions. Legul still hadn't been able to uncover anything.

"—Pardon me, Master Legul." Just then, one of his own subordinates entered the room. "We've received a report from our spies."

"Anything about the Rainbow Crown?"

"No, a separate matter. We've received word that a foreign delegation has been staying with Voras for several days."

"A foreign delegation?"

In Patura, there were six figures who worked for the *Ladu*—the sea teachers, called *Kelil*. Voras was the oldest *Kelil*, who'd been serving the Zarif since the previous *Ladu*. Although his fleet was small, it was powerful. Legul couldn't take him lightly.

"Where exactly is the delegation from?"

"We cannot say for certain, but we have reason to believe they're from Soljest. We have confirmed one of its leaders is among the group."

"Soljest, huh…?"

Legul started to think. *Could Voras have called on them in the middle of this mess?*

Something wasn't adding up. The delegation was arriving much too soon. Its visit must be pure coincidence.

But what would happen if Voras asked Soljest for aid?

I can't imagine Soljest will intervene. They have no obligation to go to such lengths to save Patura, and they gain nothing from it. Even if they do send reinforcements, I'll have everything settled by the time they arrive from their far-Northern nation.

The subordinate continued. "We've received a report that the delegation is looking for someone."

"Looking for someone? Alois or Felite?"

"Someone else, apparently. We don't have the details, but a member of the delegation fell overboard during their journey. Our guess is that this person is of incredibly high standing."

"……"

For some reason, Legul found himself thinking about the young man he had seen in a jail cell several days prior. The prisoner had had the audacity to ask Legul's men to fill his cell with stuff, and he hadn't faltered under Legul's gaze. But according to a subordinate's report, he was just a merchant from Soljest.

"…Send someone to the jail immediately. There's another prisoner besides Felite. Bring him here."

"What?" The subordinate hesitated for a second before nodding. "I mean, yes, sir. Understood."

"Pardon me!" The doors burst open, slammed open by another soldier.

"We just received an urgent message from the guards! The prisoners have escaped!"

"*What?!*" Legul stared at him before whipping over to look out the window.

Outside the fortress, in the darkness of night, the wind was starting to pick up.

Wein's rescue group had slipped out of the fortress and was headed to an empty beach away from the facility.

"Your Highness, please watch your step."

"I know." Wein glanced to the side, eyeing Felite, who had been hoisted onto a soldier's back. He was still unconscious, and it didn't seem like he'd stir anytime soon.

Wein wasn't sure if they'd be able to treat him in time.

The group arrived at its destination: a midsize boat where a group of people were waiting for them.

"Ah, you've all returned."

They looked at the rescue team, tense expressions melting with joy and relief.

"We were able to save His Highness, thanks to you," Ninym replied.

"Then this person must be…"

"Yes, this is His Highness, Prince Wein," Ninym introduced, and the prince stepped forward.

The members of the other party immediately dropped to their knees.

"It's an honor to make your acquaintance, Prince Wein. We're…"

"Merchants of Salendina, right?" He took their hands one by one. "You were the reason I was able to escape. I'm eternally grateful."

"Please… We do not deserve your thanks." Their shoulders trembled. "It is nothing compared to the kindness the royal family has extended to us Flahm."

The Flahm. Each person now kneeling before him was one. Salendina Company was run by Flahm.

I never imagined they'd help me in this way.

Of course, Wein had known about the company even before everything went down. Salendina didn't operate on a large scale—most of its wares went to Patura's central island, which allowed it connections everywhere on the archipelago. He'd figured Ninym would go to these people for help, refusing to give up on her search.

That was why he'd leveraged the ransom to make the guards contact the company. Sure enough, this had tipped off Ninym that Wein had been captured by Legul's fleet and taken to the fortress. With the merchants, she'd quietly crept toward the fortress by ship, pinpointed Wein's location by the cloth flapping against the iron bars, and waited for a particularly blustery day that would mask any sound as they went in to rescue him.

"I was planning to meet in an official capacity with the mighty clan in the South. I'm sorry for putting you in danger on your home turf."

"What are you saying?" A man shook his head. "I heard that our ancestors, like all other Flahm, were oppressed by the state. I'm sure your kingdom was a beacon of hope as they traversed the barren wilderness to make their way to the North. Now, after all these years, there is no greater honor than being able to look upon the countenance of His Highness, who carries the blood of those great kings, to say nothing of helping save his life."

The Flahm wasn't exaggerating. There had been a time when Natra was the only nation to treat the Flahm as people. At present, the influence of the Empire had made the eastern half of the continent follow suit. A future in Natra must have been the thing that had given the Flahm hope.

"But won't this put Salendina in a tough position?"

"You need not worry. We're used to being shunned. In fact, we're prepared to go into hiding at any moment. As long as our people are safe, we can wait until things calm down and start business anew."

"I see... I promise to reward you once everything is over."

"Understood. We would be most grateful."

The Flahm bowed their heads low.

A soldier called out, "Your Highness, we are prepared for departure."

"I see. Well, then— Hmm?" Wein suddenly felt something behind him and glanced over his shoulder.

He saw flickering flames weaving through the darkness. The fortress torches. There were more of them lit than before the escape. It seemed they'd been found out somehow.

"We better get going. Ninym, where to?" Wein asked, clambering aboard.

"The vessel and its crew are under the protection of Princess Tolcheila's acquaintance, who goes by the name of Voras. We should return there for now and consider our next steps."

"Voras... One of those powerful *Kelil* leaders, right? Sounds good. Let's get going."

"—Wait."

Everyone stopped in their tracks. Their eyes all shifted toward Felite, whom a soldier had been trying to carry onto the boat.

"You're awake," Wein said. "Sorry for taking you without permission."

Felite offered a weak smile. "I'm grateful for that, so don't apologize—Prince Wein."

So he knew Wein was the prince. He had either overheard their conversation or connected the dots himself.

"I must warn you of the ship's destination. I will be frank: You should not go to Voras."

"Why?"

"Because of the wind." Felite pointed up to the sky, wincing. The pain from the wounds he'd received during his interrogation must have been coming back. "The winds at this time of year…turn into storms. If you try to go to Voras's island, you'll be rendered immobile halfway. Meaning there is a good chance Legul's fleet will catch up and capture us."

"A storm, huh…?" Wein took in the sky.

The stars had dimmed under the clouds rolling in. The wind was still blowing, but Wein wasn't sure if it would grow into a full-blown storm. But Felite's opinion, as that of an island native, was worth taking into consideration.

"What should we do if a storm is coming? It's not like we can stay here, right?"

Felite pointed. "Go east. I have a hideout on a small island there. It's only known to me and a few others. Our pursuers won't find us, and we should…be able…to ride out the…"

"Ah, hey!"

Felite fainted before finishing his sentence.

"…What do you think, Your Highness?"

Should they go to Voras or Felite's hideout?

Wein considered Ninym's question for a few seconds.

"We'll go east."

They boarded the ship, ready to sail across the sea in the darkness of night.

Chapter 3 | Rainbow Crown

The morning sun flooded the island with many colors.

Its shadows seemed inkier in contrast.

The faces of boulders and the forests glowed white with light. Darkness stretched out behind them. The rays that passed through the tree branches fanned across the ground like white arrows.

"Has the storm passed?" Wein murmured, holding up his hand against the light streaming from the window of his room.

They were in a house in the forest, built in a hollow that couldn't be seen from the ocean—a proper hideout.

They had arrived there in the dead of night. Just as Felite had predicted, a storm had turned the sea into thrashing waves. They'd reached this island just as things were taking a turn for the worse.

They'd concealed the boat in the shadow of a boulder and set forth until they found this house. After determining this was Felite's hideout, the group had spent the rest of the night holed up in here.

"Well, then..."

Wein rose from the bed, stretching his limbs gently. No issues there. He left the room and met a soldier patrolling the hallway.

"Good morning, Your Highness." The soldier immediately bowed.

Wein nodded in approval. "Thanks for keeping an eye out. Anything out of the ordinary?"

"No. Fortunately, all has been calm." The soldier's face started to cloud over. "However, because we lack proper manpower, I cannot say our security is infallible. It is best if we leave as soon as possible and rejoin the rest of the group."

"I can't argue with that…"

They had only three people who could serve as guards, one of them being Ninym. Even if they worked in shifts, it would pose major difficulties. The two Flahm accompanying them were the sailors who'd handled the ship and had no battle training. They could undertake the role of guard in a pinch, but it certainly wasn't optimal.

"And where's Ninym?"

"She has not yet left the room next door, so it is my understanding that she is still asleep."

This was surprising. Since Ninym almost always woke up earlier than Wein, he'd figured this day would be no different.

"I hope I am not out of line for revealing this, but Lady Ninym has not had much sleep since you fell overboard. I think the exhaustion hit when she confirmed your safety."

"Ah…I see. That makes sense."

It wasn't hard to imagine the anguish that had tormented her after her master fell into the sea. He had been able to kick back in his jail cell only because he'd known their ship hadn't been captured. If it had either been seized or gone missing, he would have been pacing in his cell.

"Of course, we were all anxious over Your Highness's safety. I realize I'm a bit late in saying so, but I am so relieved you are safe."

"I'm sorry about that. I guess I was pretty reckless."

"I will fall into the sea in your stead next time."

"I'll try and be more careful so there is no next time. I think I'll go check on her." Wein knocked lightly on the door next to his. No answer.

"I'm coming in." He nudged open the door.

The room was simple, like Wein's. There were almost no furnishings in the hideout, and the room was outfitted with only a simple bookshelf and a bed.

Ninym was fast asleep—deep in her dreams. She didn't even respond when he stepped into her room. He drew near, gently stroking her hair.

He'd caused her to worry so much, but he was glad things had turned out the way they had. Wein wasn't sure what would have happened if Ninym had been captured by those pirates.

He didn't doubt Ninym would have found some genius way to escape their grasp, too. Maybe even by stealing a ship.

In the end, he did not regret his snap judgment to rescue her.

…If my old self saw me, I bet he'd think I'd gone off the deep end.

Though he was still a greenhorn in the eyes of society, there was a time when he had been even more immature.

It wasn't that he had been a teenage rebel. In fact, he had been just the opposite. He'd been reserved, and he'd done what others expected of him. It had been as if he had no heart at all.

Humans were truly unpredictable creatures, especially if a single girl could totally transform him. For better or worse, people could change. Wein was no exception.

He could say with confidence he'd changed for the better. It was impossible to imagine Ninym would be a bad influence on him.

If there was anyone who dared to suggest she was…well, they would need to prepare to become his mortal enemy.

"Mmm…" Ninym quietly slurred in her sleep. "Wein…"

Was she dreaming of him? He caressed her cheek as if to reassure her.

She tenderly placed her hand over his…

"—There's still more work to do."

Wein yanked away his hand on reflex.

…But not before she closed in on him, hugging his neck tightly.

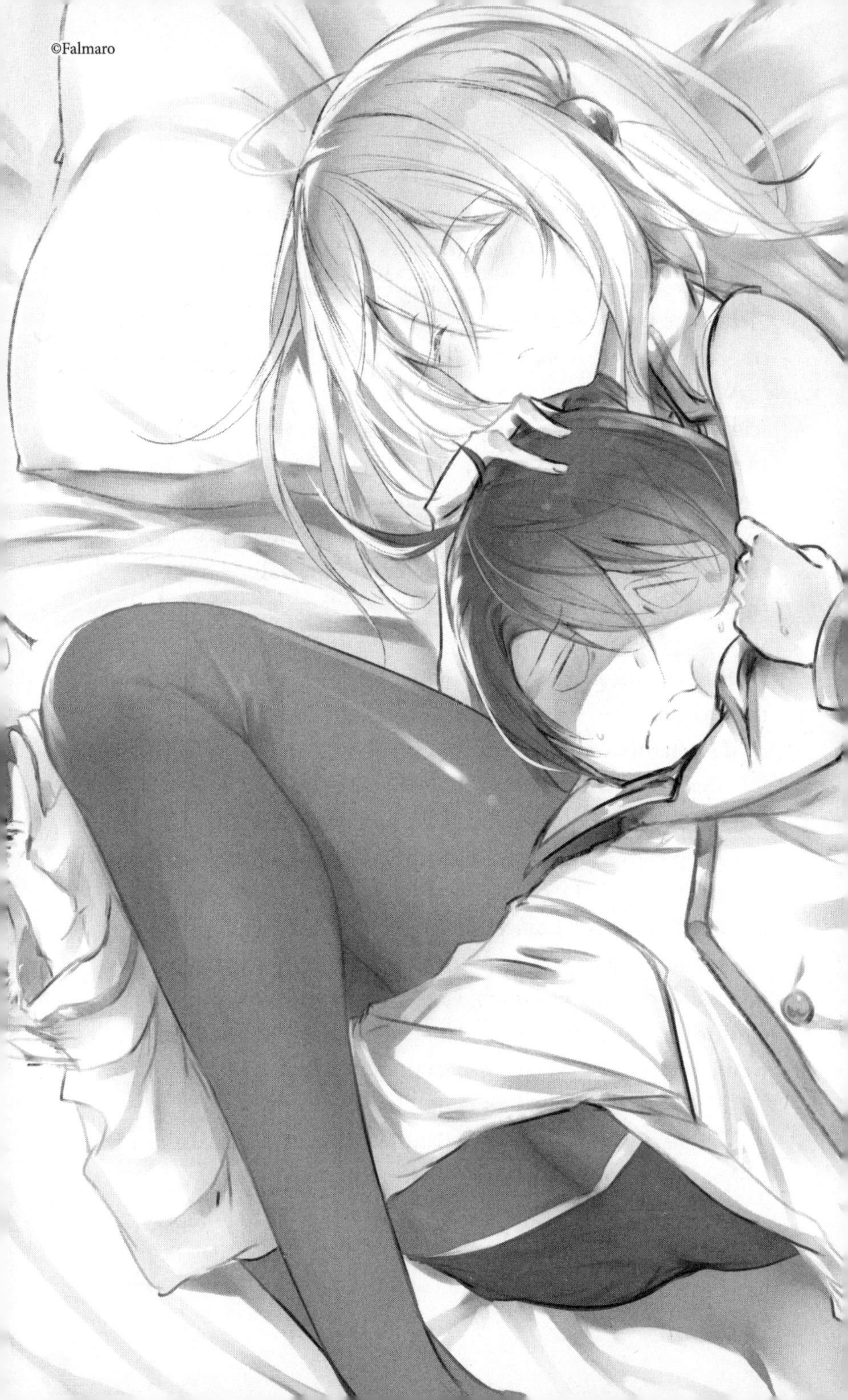

"Ngh! Miss Ninym! I can't breathe! You're suffocating me!"

"Zzz… If you don't finish in five minutes…I'll choke you to death…"

"Five minutes? I won't last five seconds like this! Wake up! Please! Get up! Miss Ninym!"

"Zzz…"

Wein thrashed around, desperately trying to undo her unconscious choke hold.

"Aaaaah…" Ninym yawned, enjoying the warm weather.

She slowly came to her senses, stretching out her limbs to wake them up. Her body felt light. It had been a long time since she'd slept so soundly.

Had she overslept? Ninym was about to jump out of bed to check the time.

"…Wein? What are you doing?"

Just then, she found Wein lying across the floor and breathing feebly.

"Nothing… I came to check on you since you weren't up yet…"

"Ah, I knew I overslept. I'm sorry. You know, you shouldn't just enter a girl's room when she's getting her beauty sleep."

"I'll take that to heart…" he answered weakly as she admonished him with a flushed face.

Had he been exercising? What a strange master she had.

Ninym ordered him to wait outside, shoving him from the room before fixing herself up. A bath would have been nice, but such luxuries weren't available in their current situation.

She left her room, ready to start the day.

"Thank you for waiting, Your Highness."

"It was like walking on clouds, compared to those five minutes of hell."

What in the world was he talking about?

"Let us see to your breakfast. We have access to some preserved foods, fortunately, so we will be able to prepare something in no time at all. I should mention it will be modest fare."

"I'm not going to order anyone to bring in something gourmet in our circumstances."

"I'm terribly sorry," Ninym said. "After your meal, we will discuss what lies ahead. I am concerned about Felite's condition…"

The patrol guard's ears perked up. "We received a report from the seamen while you were both sleeping. His condition is stable, and he's expected to take a turn for the better with some rest, though we cannot say when he will wake."

"I see. I'm glad to hear it," Wein responded.

Felite was being looked after by Flahm sailors after having been carried to the hideout, which was stocked with medicine and food. Felite, mercifully, was able to receive the treatment he needed.

"I'll see how he's doing later…which means I've got some time to kill until breakfast."

"We're being chased. I imagine we'll undergo some unexpected trials. It would be best if Your Highness is nourished so you may act quickly should anything happen."

In other words, Ninym was telling Wein to stay put.

There really wasn't anything for the prince to do. Wein knew wandering around would just cause the guards more trouble.

"In that case…I think I'll go check out *that* room."

"'That room'…? Ah yes. I think that would be the perfect place to pass the time."

Wein nodded.

It was the best time to check out the library farther within the hideout.

The room wasn't marked by a special nameplate, but it was obvious it was a library based on the heaps of books that filled the room.

"I'll be standing guard outside."

"Thanks."

With the guard posted outside the door, Wein began his hunt.

The great room was lined with bookshelves, though not nearly enough to contain all the thick tomes. They were set in piles on the floor—heaps of bound books and bundles of paper loosely tied together.

"Hmm, it looks like most of these are on the history of Patura. This one has its...mythology? It's about the sea god Auvert, who carried a golden spear and white-silver shield and wore the shining Rainbow Crown. Patura's central deity, huh."

Wein had always been a bookworm. All his vassals knew that about him. His motivation to read was simple: It was another way to study.

Wein was crown prince and regent of Natra—positions in which he juggled several governmental responsibilities, including those that were financial, tax related, legal, military, and diplomatic. Though he consulted his vassals about these matters, it was Wein who had to make the final call. How high should taxes be raised? What sorts of wages should people be paid? What should they do if there was a famine?

How did he make these decisions?

In personal situations, instinct was enough for a snap judgment. In matters of national politics, however, even a single bill could affect thousands of subjects. Intuition just didn't cut it.

That was where the collected documents on the history of Natra came in.

They chronicled the effects of certain laws on citizens, tax systems on military profits and uprisings, military budget cuts on coups.

These records were a huge help to politicians.

There was no question Wein was a great prince. But the teen royal had been able to become a ruler only because he'd studied up on the two hundred years of government decisions in the history of the Kingdom of Natra.

"Here is a sea chart of Patura. This paper documents changes in ocean climate... Oh, this is on the advancement of their ships. I'm interested in that one."

For this reason, reading documents was a habit of his. He hadn't had time to come here when they'd arrived last night, but he'd had his eye on this place the entire time.

"Interesting... It's unexpected, really. I knew the island nation was going to be different from Natra, but how did they manage to keep such pristine records...?"

Wein suddenly felt a breeze on his face. He looked around to see that a window nearby was open. Worried that papers might blow around everywhere, he went to close it—and saw something.

Wet footprints on the window frame.

"_____"

Were they still around? They had to be.

Whoever it was had looked for an opening in the patrol and had sneaked in before Wein got to the library. Wein must have come strolling into the room as they lurked in the shadows.

The guard is outside this room. Even if I call him and he rushes to stand in front of me—he won't make it in time.

Wein could feel someone behind him. They must have realized he knew they were there.

This is bad. He didn't even have a short sword on him.

Wein inhaled.

"Enemy attack!" yelled the prince, flinging the book in his hand behind him.

"Gwagh?!" Someone grunted. The tome had hit its target.

Wein wasted no time taking cover behind a nearby bookshelf and rummaging to find another book to throw.

"Don't touch those, servant! Everything in here belongs to the young master!"

Wein's hand froze in place—for two reasons. First, because the intruder had referred to a "young master," and second, because his opponent sounded like a young girl.

"Your Highness!" The guard flew into the room. His eyes caught sight of a girl wielding a short sword at Wein. He unsheathed his own blade without hesitation and swung at her.

"*Hah—!*"

The guard cut through some bookshelves, tomes and all, but the girl wasn't in his line of attack. She kicked off the wall, flying to another shelf, barely grazing the ceiling.

Her eyes were focused not on the guard but rather on Wein. She'd realized he'd make a valuable hostage.

Wein faced her. "—Wait! We're not your enemy!"

"Don't mess with me!" Nothing could stop her. She kicked off the shelf and closed in on him.

The guard stepped in. "Your Highness! Please stay back!"

"No! Put away your swords, both of you! This is some sort of misunderstanding!"

"Now is not the time to be saying that!"

Wein clicked his tongue in annoyance. How could he put an end to this?

If the fight went on, it would just end in meaningless casualties.

Two human-shaped shadows loomed in the open doorway.

"Your Highness!"

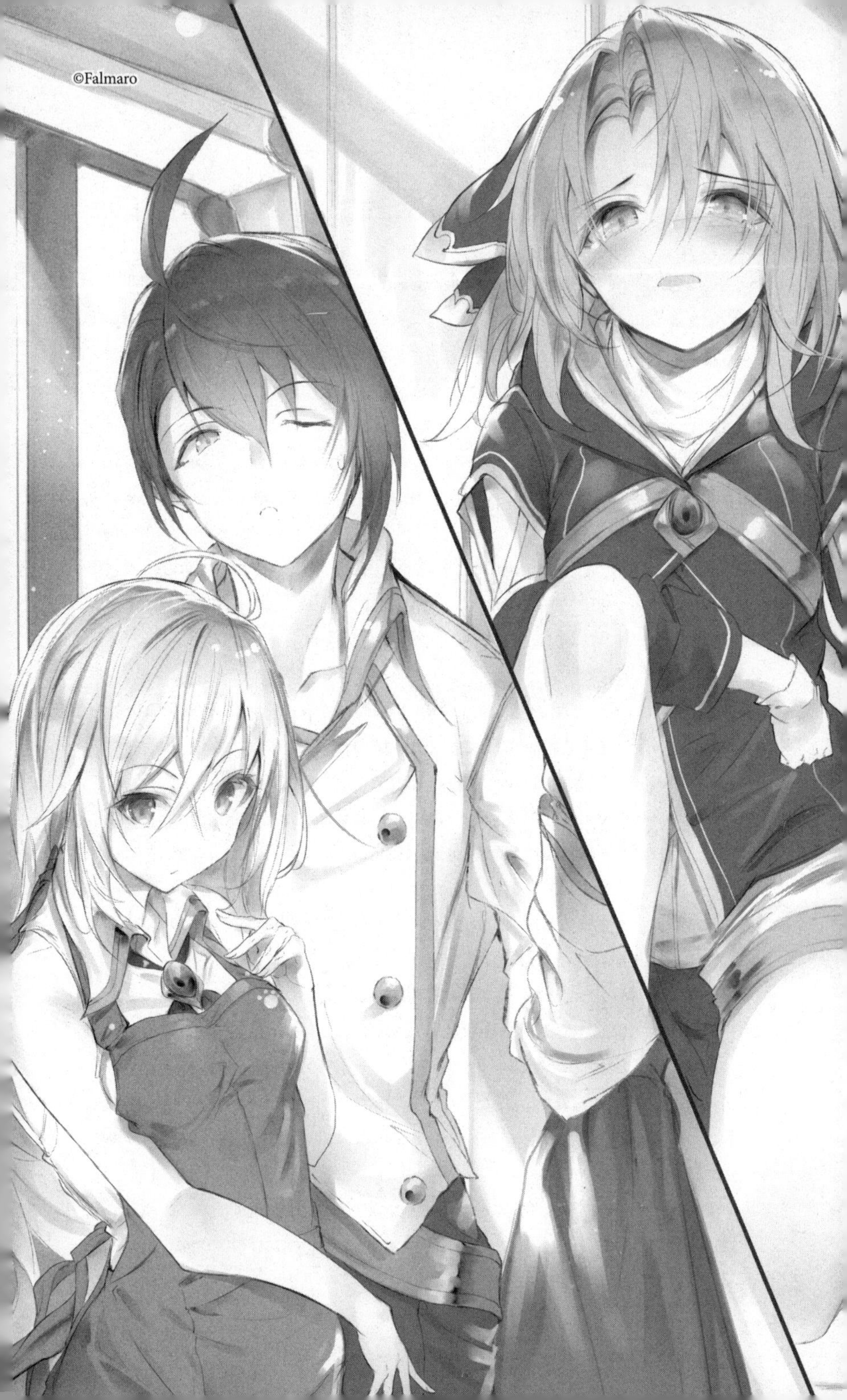
©Falmaro

Ninym, still in her apron. She must have heard the commotion while preparing breakfast and come running.

Next to her, another shadow called out, "Apis!"

The girl turned around, caught off guard. Her eyes reflected the sight of Felite leaning against a wall.

"Put down your sword. I'm fine. They aren't enemies."

His admonition was affectionate.

The short sword in Apis's hand dropped to the floor. Lips trembling, she dashed over to Felite and knelt before him.

"Young master! I'm relieved to see you're okay...!"

"I'm glad to see you safe, too, Apis," Felite assured the trembling girl, cooing in a gentle voice.

Wein and the guard exchanged glances. He gave a wordless order to the guard to sheathe his sword, and he obeyed, nodding in understanding.

Ninym wasn't sure how to respond for a little bit. She was still trying to process all of this.

"It seems I'll need to prepare more breakfast," she noted.

"I'm terribly sorry for my disgraceful behavior. I had no idea you were the Prince of Natra."

Wein had proposed they have breakfast first, even though they had a great deal to discuss. All parties scarfed down Ninym's meal until they were modestly full. Felite's servant Apis immediately bowed her head when they were done.

"To think I raised a sword against the one who saved Master Felite... I'm ashamed."

Felite had his head bowed, too. "The fault lies with me. I should have considered and kept you informed of the possibility that she might either be here or arrive while we were on this island. I hope you'll forgive me."

Wein nodded, sitting across from them. "The situation called for it. I don't blame you."

Felite had been too exhausted to hold a simple conversation with Wein. It would have been unfair to expect him to anticipate Apis in his condition.

Of course, Ninym appeared reluctant to forgive anyone who had raised a sword against Wein, even in the current circumstances. He gave her a look, however, warning her to keep herself in check, with which she reluctantly complied. If Wein had received so much as the slightest scratch, things would have gone south. Luckily for everyone, they'd managed to settle things without injury.

"There's something more constructive we could be discussing," Wein said.

Felite nodded. "You're right. Let's break down the situation. As you know, I am Felite Zarif, the second son of Alois. I was captured by my older brother during his raid and thrown in prison as Alois died in the chaos."

"And I am the prince of Natra, who came to meet Alois to negotiate a trade deal. I was caught by Legul's patrol ship and taken prisoner. I bet you never expected a foreign prince to be in the cell right next to you."

"Indeed… So you really are Prince Wein."

"Sorry for lying. I couldn't tell a stranger of my identity in our situation."

"I completely understand." Felite turned his gaze to his servant. "Apis, I must ask you: Why did you come to this island on your own? I thought I instructed you to bring the islands' leaders together."

"……" She looked troubled, suddenly kneeling before him. Her

voice was strained. "I'm so sorry... I have betrayed your faith in me...!"

Wein and Ninym looked at one another.

Felite closed his eyes tightly. "So you've lost...the Rainbow Crown."

"Yes...! I am so sorry...!"

The Rainbow Crown.

It had come up during Felite and Legul's conversation in jail and in the legend from the book in the library.

"It belonged to the sea god Auvert. One of Patura's great treasures, right?"

"Exactly. One hundred years ago, my ancestor and the priest at the time—Malaze—held up the Rainbow Crown before the people, presenting it as a gift from the sea god."

It was said that when light struck this treasure, it shined in all the colors of the rainbow, giving one the power to control the sea and sky as desired. Whenever other nations threatened Patura, the *Ladu* would use the Rainbow Crown to drive them off.

To someone like Wein, born and raised in Natra, the legend was dubious at best, but that wasn't the case for the people of Patura. Many of the islanders believed the Rainbow Crown held such power.

It made sense that Levetia had no leverage on these islands. To the people of Patura, this was the holy nation protected by the sea god and the power of the Rainbow Crown.

"Is the Rainbow Crown really that amazing?" Wein asked.

"Yes... Its magical power captivates those who look upon it, me included. But its ability to control sea and sky is just a hoax started by Malaze," Felite replied. "When emergency situations arose, he spread word that it was all resolved by the power of the Rainbow Crown. Whenever a storm brewed, he attributed it to the treasure. It didn't take long for the islanders to come around and accept that as truth. Over a hundred years, it's become a symbol of Patura."

Everything was to cement the Zarif's authority. As long as the people thought the Rainbow Crown was blessed with the power of the god, the Zarif could command these waters.

Wein thought it was a brilliant strategy. Something like that was easier said than done. There had to be periods when it seemed as if the crown might lose its hold on the people—such as when it failed to deliver. Even so, this little hoax held strong even after a century and multiple generations. The Rainbow Crown continued to own its prestige. But there was something ironic about this whole thing.

The Rainbow Crown had been stolen because it had tricked the people a little too well.

"Who was the traitor, Apis?"

"...Sir Rodolphe," she answered, almost in a whisper. "Because you acted as the bait, young master, I was able to take the Rainbow Crown and escape Legul and his pursuers. However, his subordinates were keeping watch on Sir Voras, whose aid you initially requested. I couldn't make contact with him..."

"So you entrusted it to Rodolphe." Felite looked up at the ceiling. After a few seconds of silence, he looked at Wein and explained. "Rodolphe has supported the Zarif for a long, long time. He is one of the *Kelil*, trusted by my father... It seems he's been entranced by the magic of the Rainbow Crown..."

"Yes..." Apis agreed. "He readily agreed to help you when I brought him the crown, but he's abandoned you now, plotting to make himself the next *Ladu* as soon as Legul and the other *Kelil* crush each other..."

"We may have safely made our escape, but we can't trust anyone now that Rodolphe has betrayed us. Now that the Rainbow Crown has been stolen, it'll be difficult to unite the people under me. I imagine you thought you could rescue me yourself and came here to prepare, right?"

"Yes... I'm so sorry, young master..." Tears rolled down Apis's cheeks. Felite gently stroked his servant's hair.

"No need to cry, Apis. This is tough, but it's not the worst that could happen. We're both safe. Let's be grateful for that." Felite turned back to Wein. "Prince Wein, that's our situation."

"Looks like you've really been driven into a corner."

"Embarrassingly so. I have no soldiers, no wealth, and no authority."

Wein could feel great power resting in Felite's gaze.

"Prince Wein, I would like to ask for your assistance in taking back the Patura Archipelago."

Wein had known this would happen.

Felite had been left to his own devices. In reality, it was worse. This was a desperate situation from which there was no escape.

After all, the foreign prince joining him at the breakfast table wasn't an ally. The two were nothing more than accidental travel partners.

"I understand that to you, Prince, this is nothing more than an unfortunate accident. No one would blame you for turning a blind eye to this situation and returning to your country. Even better, you could divulge information about the Rainbow Crown and deliver my severed head to Legul as a gift."

Apis jumped in her skin. It seemed she hadn't considered this. When she realized she'd made a gaffe, she prepared to face off against Wein, but Felite stopped her.

"You, however, have made no effort to leave. I see there is room for discussion. What do you say?"

"...You're putting me in a tough spot." Wein flashed a wry smile. "I would never imagine turning you over to Legul, but it is an option, now that you mention it."

A white lie. Wein had already taken the idea into account. He had even given the two soldiers on standby orders to be ready to rush in on Felite at any time.

"In other words, you need me to serve as your ally. Seems to me like you don't have many bargaining chips in this situation, Sir Felite. It's bold of you, but I'll show some mercy."

"Honestly, I'm so nervous, my stomach is in knots... If I may say so, I would still try to win you over as an ally even if it weren't out of necessity."

"Oh?" That certainly caught Wein's attention. "Why is that? I hate to tell you that I haven't brought any men or money with me. Even if we team up, I wouldn't expect us to be much help."

"I understand. Why don't we think of it this way? I've lost my troops, wealth, and influence...even my dignity now that I've been caught once by Legul. I'll never control these waters again unless I have your full cooperation."

"Kch." A sound escaped Wein's vocal cords.

Only Ninym realized he was trying to hold back a laugh.

Felite continued. "This is a preliminary battle. I am gauging my own skills to see if I can take on the trial imposed upon me and convince you to form an alliance with us."

The man looked straight at Wein, eyes shining with confidence.

"...Bold of you to toy with royalty to test your strength." Wein's lips curled into a smile. "All right. If you're going to go that far, I guess I can lend an ear. How will you help us?"

"As soon as we take back Patura, we will trade with you under your conditions."

"Hmm. Anything else?"

"We'll provide you with vessels and disclose our shipbuilding techniques. We can also offer instruction in seamanship."

"Wonderful. And?"

"If Natra goes to war with another nation and requires a naval fleet, we will come to your aid."

"Yes, yes, I see..." Wein nodded. "It's not *nearly enough*."

He completely shut Felite down.

"A feast of empty promises is fine and all, but you're only talking about after you've beaten Legul. You don't have enough resources to make me believe in your victory."

It was a cold refusal, but Felite didn't recoil.

"I understand where you're coming from. That is why I will provide one last offering."

"Oh, and what might that be?"

"*The history of the Zarif,*" he replied. "I will give you everything the Zarif has recorded about Patura."

"———" Wein's eyes widened. His reaction encouraged Felite to continue.

"If the rumors about you are true, you will understand the value of my offer. In truth, that library is filled with information on the island, written by the Zarif, including yours truly. I will use those records to take down Legul."

Felite had aimed for the right spot.

The royal family of Natra had two hundred years of accumulated history. That was precisely why Wein understood the value in such a blessing.

"...Why would you give us something so important?"

"The authority of the Rainbow Crown has grown too powerful. It's only misled the islanders—and the Zarif themselves. It makes such documents seem unnecessary. I've been preserving them because I believe they represent the real hopes of the Zarif."

He took a deep breath.

"Well, Wein Salema Arbalest? Vessels! Men! Skills! History! Am I worthy enough for you to take your chances on me?!"

The room was silent. Apis and Ninym looked at their masters, gulping.

After an agonizing moment of silence, Wein spoke up. "...I'd like to know what you're planning to do next."

"I'll need the Rainbow Crown if I hope to build a group against Legul. To make that happen, I'll contact some *Kelil* behind closed doors. There's a detailed sea chart of Patura among our documents, along with information about the *Kelil*. I'll use those to seek aid and steal the Rainbow Crown back from Rodolphe."

"It won't work." Wein shut down Felite's plan on the spot. "We'd be too late by then. As we're bogged down by the task of persuading each of the *Kelil*, Legul will get his ships and rip the crown from Rodolphe's hands."

"Ngh..." Felite was rendered speechless.

Wein turned to his aide. "Ninym, bring the sea charts and every document on the *Kelil* from the library."

"Yes, understood." Ninym immediately jumped up to leave the room.

"Prince Wein... What are you...?" Felite looked stumped.

"You've shown me your value, Sir Felite." Wein turned to the man, beaming at him.

"Now it's my turn to prove myself a worthy ally."

In the future, Felite Zarif would come to record this day in the history book of the Zarif:

On this day, in a small hideaway that draws no attention, I secured the continent's greatest ally.

"—They're late!"

The northwestern Patura Archipelago.

In a room of a mansion built on one of the many scattered islands, Tolcheila seemed positively perturbed.

"Curses! When does Prince Wein plan on coming back?!"

Tolcheila had heard he'd safely escaped Legul's stronghold. It was only natural that he should seek refuge with them—except he still hadn't shown his face around these parts.

"Voras! Didn't you say the rescue mission was a success?!" Tolcheila glared next to her, stiffening her posture.

A man named Voras sat elegantly, balancing a book in one hand. He was one of the *Kelil*. Though he was an elderly gentleman, his back was as straight and solid as an evergreen. He had a gentle demeanor, but nothing about him was senile.

"Dear me. That was certainly what my subordinates told me," Voras responded as he looked down at his book. He was like a grandfather dismissing his granddaughter's mood swings. "I imagine they're hiding away on a small island somewhere to escape their pursuers. There are plenty of such hideaways across Patura, after all."

"Nghhhh… That prince and his little band of followers are out of control! I will be in trouble if I don't return home quickly…!"

Aside from the few personnel who had gone to rescue Wein, almost everyone who had been accompanying the prince and his personal retinue was under Tolcheila's command. Even so, the fact that they'd left Wein in the sea, prioritizing Tolcheila, didn't sit well with her. Though she'd heard of his successful escape, the princess hadn't yet been able to confirm the sovereign's safety with her own two eyes. She was stewing in fear, on pins and needles, ready for them to burst in at any moment.

"Come, Lady Tolcheila. I'm certain they have their reasons. Worrying will not help. For now, let us be patient."

"If I could get even a second of rest, I wouldn't be so pressed! Besides, Voras, don't you feel helpless in this situation, too?! How can you be so at ease?!"

Legul had taken control of the central island. Even Tolcheila knew his influence was growing by the day. Voras *should* have been busy dealing with the situation, but the old man was wasting time as if nothing were extraordinary about this situation.

"There's a storm brewing within Patura. Be that as it may, worrying won't help, as I just said. We quietly wait for the tide to change."

"And if we're swallowed up before it changes?!"

"Then we shall become seaweed, floating in the waves. For those born and raised by the sea, no death is more fitting."

"Tch…! No wonder you get along with my father…!"

Tolcheila was under Voras's protection because of his personal friendship with King Gruyere.

During one of Gruyere's previous visits to the islands, Voras had been personally selected to entertain him. They seemed to be on the same wavelength and hit it off right away. Together, they commanded their fleets and defeated nearby pirates while guzzling booze.

"Regardless of what happens, I shall ensure your escape, Lady Tolcheila. You may rest easy in that regard. If you are still unnerved, why not read a book?" Voras motioned to the one in his hand. "I'm quite fond of this one. It is the legend of how the sea god takes his golden spear and white-silver shield and defeats the dragon terrorizing local waters."

"I have not the faintest interest!" Tolcheila snapped. Voras cracked a wry smile. "I've had enough! If this is how it'll be, I'll cook every last bit of food in our stores to distract myself!"

"Ha-ha-ha, I'm certain King Gruyere would be jealous of my position, treated to your cooking, Princess Tolcheila."

Storming away from Voras, Tolcheila headed for the kitchen.

Just then, a messenger came rushing in.

"Pardon me! I have an urgent message for you, Sir Voras!"

"Calm yourself. There is no need to panic… What is it?"

"Yes, well—"

Tolcheila was stunned at the news.

"It appears," Voras murmured quietly, "that the tides have changed."

"Did you just say you know where the Rainbow Crown is?!"

Several days had passed since Felite escaped his cell. Legul had cast a wide search net, yet he'd come up empty. He couldn't hide his frustration anymore.

Legul jumped to his feet when the subordinate gave his report.

"Where?!" he demanded. "Where is it?!"

"Yes, well, we do not have an exact location yet. However, there is a very good chance that it is currently in the possession of Rodolphe."

"Rodolphe… That guy…"

Rodolphe's image flashed in Legul's mind. He was one of the *Kelil* trusted by Alois Zarif. Their last encounter had been before Legul was exiled from Patura. If Rodolphe was still alive, he had to be an old man like Voras.

"You're sure it's not Voras?"

"Yes. Rumors have been circulating that Rodolphe has been hiding it. We conducted our investigations and obtained several testimonials that say they saw Rodolphe with the treasure." The messenger continued. "It seems that after increasing his number of ships, he locked himself away in his mansion, refusing a public appearance since. Eyewitnesses say they saw someone who looked like Apis carrying out operations nearby. She had a large bundle with her."

"Hmm..."

Based on the current situation, it wasn't strange for anyone to expand their battle forces.

But Apis's appearance was a key clue. She was Felite's trusted retainer, and Legul hadn't been able to find her during the raid. This was enough to make them believe that Felite had entrusted her with the Rainbow Crown.

There were some things that weren't adding up.

"...Has Voras done anything?"

"Nothing in particular to report at the moment..."

"Tch. What's that grandpa thinking?"

Legul had expected Felite to join up with Voras, mostly because of that young man who had escaped with his brother. He seemed like a key player in Soljest and had run off almost as soon as Legul had caught him. Apparently, the intermediary company that was going to pay the ransom had slipped away. If the two men had been able to act so swiftly, the escape must have been the other man's idea. Felite was just a lucky extra.

The escaped man would have headed for the delegation vessel currently docked at Voras's place, and Felite wouldn't object to asking for help from a *Kelil*. Once he was under Voras's protection, they would try to collect the Rainbow Crown.

Legul had planned on stopping them there. He'd never imagined Rodolphe would be in possession of it!

"Was Felite seen at Rodolphe's?"

"That has not been confirmed."

"......"

The Rainbow Crown was there. Felite was not. There was radio silence from Rodolphe's end. He hadn't even launched an attack on Legul.

If he were planning to go up against me, he would be endorsing Felite and coming forward with the Rainbow Crown. Instead, he's trying to keep the crown a secret… Did he kill Felite to take it for himself?

It was possible. Legul wasn't the only one with motives. In fact, he thought everyone in Patura wanted the Rainbow Crown.

The messenger was ready to back up his theory. "We haven't investigated this enough, but we've noticed some activity from the other *Kelil*. They must have received similar information and are planning on taking the crown for themselves."

"…Guess we've got no time to waste."

There was something that bothered him. The rumors of the crown being with Rodolphe seemed suspicious. Maybe they were trying to get a reaction out of him.

Who was behind this? Felite, Voras, or someone else? He thought it over for a moment, but he immediately stopped himself. It wasn't as if he understood everything about Patura; he had been exiled and returned only recently. Naturally, Legul had researched things for his plan, but some information is impossible to know without lived experiences. Asking any more pointless questions that had no answers would be a waste of time.

"Whoever it is, we'll just crush them all."

Legul had to prove himself. Prove that he, the exiled Legul Zarif, was the absolute ruler of the Patura islands. Once Legul got the Rainbow Crown, he would destroy every *Kelil* loyal to Alois. Then everyone would realize banishing him had been a terrible mistake!

"Prepare the ships," Legul barked. "I'll annihilate Rodolphe and get my hands on the Rainbow Crown!"

It was like a rainbow had been locked away in a seashell.

Red. Blue. Yellow. Green. Bits of rainbow scattered in the spiral shell, colorful shards of light overlapping and winking within. It took everyone's breath away.

Even the dim room couldn't dull its brilliance.

The Rainbow Crown. Every citizen of this archipelago considered it a national treasure.

Even beasts held their breath at the sight of the crown. It possessed a certain magic.

"How beautiful..."

Drunk on its beauty, a man stood by the Rainbow Crown as if in servitude.

Rodolphe. He was one of the six *Kelil* and the possessor of the Rainbow Crown.

"It's mine... This radiance is finally mine."

Rodolphe had first seen the Rainbow Crown as a child. He'd been a pirate at the time. His parents had abandoned him, and he'd been on the verge of starvation when the pirates took him in as an apprentice.

They were vulgar and violent but chummy, treating him well. To an orphan like Rodolphe, the pirates had been family. He'd thought he'd fight by their sides forever and go on wild adventures.

In the end, however, he had destroyed that future for himself.

When he was captured by the fleet of Patura that arrived to suppress the pirates, the *Ladu* had led him away.

That was when Rodolphe saw the Rainbow Crown.

He felt electrified. Even when he tried to peel his eyes away, it kept drawing him back in.

"From today forward," the *Ladu* had told him, *"the Rainbow Crown is your master. Serve, attend, and devote yourself to it."*

He tried to refuse, but he couldn't make a sound. The Rainbow Crown seemed to become brighter. It felt like the light was alive, worming its way into his eyes. Its glow flooded his brain, whispering sweetly into his ear.

"—*Sell out your friends.*"

Rodolphe found himself revealing the location of his pirate family.

They were all caught and executed, and he was exiled for some time.

Rodolphe, however, felt neither sadness nor regret. After all, he'd done as his master wished.

After that, he polished his skills as a seaman as if possessed until he became a *Kelil*. He had neither loyalty to the elders nor love for his country. He did it solely to serve his master.

When Alois suddenly died and Apis came to Rodolphe with the Rainbow Crown, the colorful voice spoke to him again.

"—*Take control of everything.*"

Rodolphe had no objections.

"I won't hand it over to anyone. This shall be forever mine..." he murmured as he caressed the treasure. He showed none of the acumen that had supported the former *Ladu*. It wasn't necessary to fake it anymore.

"Sir Rodolphe!"

The door opened with a bang. A subordinate tumbled in.

"...I recall saying no one is to come in here."

The look in Rodolphe's eyes was bloodcurdling. The man instinctively flinched.

"I-I'm terribly sorry. We received a report that Legul's fleet is heading for this island...!"

"...So he's here."

Rodolphe's face slackened. He had known it wouldn't be long before word spread that he had the Rainbow Crown. He'd been secretly planning to use the treasure to lead a group against Legul. It seemed, however, that he was too late.

"Is the fleet ready?"

"Yes. We're ready to depart at any time."

"Good. Make sure everyone is at their stations. I'll be there shortly."

The subordinate hurried out of the room.

Alone once again, Rodolphe murmured, annoyed, "That damn upstart… He thinks he's a big shot because he got rid of Alois?"

His eyes turned to the Rainbow Crown. This invaluable treasure had to be Legul's objective. He was going to try to steal it, even though it had chosen Rodolphe!

"I ought to teach him a lesson. I will be the next ruler of Patura."

The Rainbow Crown continued to shine—either celebrating his victory or presaging his destruction.

One fleet led by Legul. Another directed by Rodolphe.

They were facing off near Rodolphe's island fortress. Twenty ships for Legul. Fifteen for Rodolphe. For a spectator, the thirty-five ships packing the waters would have been nothing short of a spectacle.

"As you might expect of a *Kelil*. Impressive military strength," Legul murmured from his flagship as he observed his opponent's battle formation.

These weren't all the ships in Legul's arsenal, but the other *Kelil* were always looking for any break in his defenses. That meant he had to leave some ships behind to defend the home base. Twenty ships were about the best he could do.

"Sir Legul, our opponent's fleet appears to be primarily galleys."

"So it would seem. Well, that's hardly surprising."

Modern ships were separated into two categories: galleys and sailing ships. The former were long, narrow, and leaflike, a dozen yards in length. A galley was outfitted with holes on each side. It was a man-powered boat that could move freely, oars shooting out of the holes as humans rowed from the inside.

On the other hand, sailing ships were rounder vessels that used wind power to push the sails attached to raised masts. Though it wasn't optimal to be at the will of the wind, there was no rowing involved. Instead, you could load up with goods and soldiers.

Of course, some galleys used sails and some sailing ships used rowers, so it wasn't as if they were completely different breeds. Sailing ships even had different sail configurations like the square rig to maximize a tailwind and the fore-and-aft rig to catch a headwind to move upwind… But ships were basically separated into galleys and sailing ships.

As for the proper choice for engaging in a battle against Patura…

"Unlike sailing ships, man-powered galleys can handle tight turns. They're rendered immobile in rough waters, but seeing how we are close to land and these waters are calm, they're the better choice—"

As Legul offered his levelheaded assessment…

"He brought sailing ships? What an idiot," Rodolphe spat, scrutinizing his opponent's formation from the galley that served as his flagship. Legul's fleet consisted of mainly sailing ships. Although the enemy was larger in number, Rodolphe knew victory was his.

The advantages of sailing ships were their load capacity and speed, which was powered by wind. They were optimal in the open sea—free of any obstacles—not the cluster of small Patura islands where the wind could cause them to crash into land. That said, strong, gusting winds didn't visit this stretch of ocean often, and they didn't last long when they did. The wind direction, however, was unpredictable. Such an environment left sailing ships without sufficient speed and made them difficult to control.

"Must be desperate after failing to gather proper sailors," commented a subordinate.

"Agreed. He wouldn't have been able to call together enough crew with the skill to run his galleys," Rodolphe replied, nodding.

For man-powered galleys to maneuver with precision, it was essential that those rowing be in time with one another. That meant skilled rowers were vital, but they were very hard to come by. Since sailing ships needed fewer people to run them, a few sailors were enough to man the vessel.

"Judging by this, he was only able to beat Alois and take over the main island by launching a surprise attack. It's sad that he was once called a child prodigy."

Rodolphe raised his hand.

"All ships prepare to attack! Let us give a proper sea burial to those fools bringing chaos to Patura!"

"Sir Legul, the enemy has begun to move."

"I can see that."

Fifteen galleys were heading toward them. Legul looked at them and snorted.

"Hmph. Stupid old man. He's been blinded by the Rainbow Crown." Legul let out an arrogant laugh. "Allow me, the blessed son of the sea, and my trained men to force you into place."

The fleets of Legul and Rodolphe. This battle would later be coined the Naval War of Patura, the prelude of the great conflict.

The curtain was rising. Enter the players.

"Are we there yet? Are we there yet?" Tolcheila repeated, kicking the bow of the ship as she stared out across the horizon.

"Now, now, there's no need to be hasty," answered Voras, acting as the captain of the ship, who was next to her. "The ocean will always be here, whether we move fast or slow."

His scolding, however, was lost on her.

"The sea might always be here, but we might miss the climax! If that happens, our efforts to come see it will all be for nothing!"

"Goodness. I didn't think you'd suggest watching a naval battle. You're just like King Gruyere."

Tolcheila was currently on a ship headed for the stretch of ocean where Legul and Rodolphe's battle was unfolding. As Voras had stated, their purpose was to spectate.

They had no intention of intervening. The light frame of their inconspicuous ship would allow them to swiftly escape if need be.

"...Hm?!" Tolcheila spotted a ship-like shadow along the horizon. She craned her neck over the edge. "Is that it?"

"It seems that way... What do we have here?"

"Can you tell who's winning?!"

Voras nodded. "—Rodolphe appears to be at a disadvantage."

"No way..."

Rodolphe was stunned by the tide of the battle.

Twenty enemy sailing ships. Fifteen galleys on his side. He had a team of trained sailors and the more maneuverable vessels. Even though he was five boats short, he should be leading them to victory...

And yet...

"Ship Number Three has capsized!"

"Ship Seven! Attacked sideboard and rendered inoperable!"

"The oars of Ship Ten and Ship Twelve have been snapped! It's impossible for them to move! They're requesting reinforcements!"

"Sir Rodolphe! We're in dire straits!"

The reports were the exact opposite of what he'd expected.

"Th-this is…"

Basic naval battle techniques said a long-range battle wasn't the answer.

For ships knocked around by the wind and waves, it was near impossible to fatally injure opposing sailors with arrows. Even if they tried to set enemy ships ablaze with fire arrows, the hulls were basically fireproof, coated with various paints to prevent rot.

Therefore, a sea battle was all about securing the spots with the best wind, striking each other with metal naval rams, and having your sailors engage in close combat.

Rodolphe had chosen to ignore the wind direction and hit his opponent with naval rams. This item that attached to the front of a ship was a destructive weapon that took advantage of the ship's momentum. This way, he could pound the enemy ship to pierce its body and stop it from moving.

But things were not going well.

Although Rodolphe's fleet could handle tight turns, it couldn't manage to catch any of the sailing ships. Plus, his vessels were being hit with naval rams. These weapons were not unique to galleys, and it hadn't escaped Rodolphe's notice that Legul's entire fleet had them.

Since the sailing ships depended on the wind, they should be having a much harder time hitting their targets than the galleys.

How were they managing to push Rodolphe's ships back?

There was only one answer to this question.

"It can't be…!" Rodolphe's lips trembled.

"He's reading the wind…!"

"Who would stand with me if I couldn't pull that off?" Legul asked, flashing a brazen smile on his flagship. "These waters are complex; the wind blows in all directions. If you can read that like the back of your hand, even a sailing ship can maneuver as well as any galley."

Of course, such a feat wasn't simple. The ability to read the subtleties of the wind and waves required either tremendous talent or long training. Legul possessed the gift, but the same could not be said of other commanding officers. It had been necessary for him to train them himself, which hadn't been easy, but Legul had been successful. He'd passed on a portion of his natural ability to his subordinates.

"It's been a dozen years since I was exiled. Did they think I was sleeping this whole time?"

He loathed Patura, the islands that had banished him. Dark motivation had helped him along the painful path he endured.

"Well, I think it's about time we deal the finishing flow. —Starboard!"

The bow of the flagship changed course.

Ahead was the ship holding Rodolphe.

"Sir Rodolphe! We've made contact with the enemy flagship!"

"Ngh…!"

The ship that carried Legul was closing in on him. It seemed confident, like the king of the sea.

"That damn neophyte…!"

Rodolphe refused to lose. The Rainbow Crown was finally in his hands. He'd never let anyone take it from him, no matter who.

"Full speed ahead toward the enemy flagship! We'll pass by and come at them from behind!"

The galley oars rowed in synchrony.

Legul's and Rodolphe's battleships. The two squared off, rushing in to close the distance between them.

Not yet. Closer…

He was at a disadvantage in terms of his ship's weight. If they collided head-on, his vessel would be the one to sustain more damage. Thus, he would have to make sure he avoided the enemy's charge, even if by a hairbreadth.

This, of course, wasn't lost on his enemy either. Whether Rodolphe chose port or starboard, the enemy ship was going to turn its bow in the same direction to crash into him.

And so he waited. The ship advanced. Rodolphe's heart felt like it might burst from his chest.

Not yet. Not yet. Not yet, not-yet-not-yet—

"—NOW! TO PORT! STOP ROWING!"

The seamen at the oars instantly obeyed his orders. The portside oars stopped midair. Only the ones on the right continued to move the boat along, letting it stray away from the left and barely skimming past the enemy flagship's right side.

Rodolphe's eyes snapped open wide. The enemy ship had stopped before him like magic.

How—? The sails!

The vision filled Rodolphe's gaze. Before he knew it, the sails of the enemy's vessel had been folded up. If they weren't unfurled, it would not be propelled forward.

Did he read my mind?!

The galley was giving the enemy vessel an uninterrupted view of its hull. If it hit with a ram now, the galley wouldn't stand a chance.

…There was still time.

This isn't over yet! Now that they've closed their sails, they're sitting ducks until they can catch the wind again!

Rodolphe's ship, made up of two levels, was equipped with more oars than the others, and it could release explosive amounts of power. There was a chance that he could put distance between them before the sailing ship had the chance to move again.

The enemy had gathered as much, springing to action to open its sails again. But before it could catch the wind again, Rodolphe gave his orders at lightning speed—

"Idiot."

That voice.

It should have disappeared in the sound of crashing waves, but Rodolphe certainly heard it coming from the bow of the enemy flagship.

Legul stood there.

"Don't you know *I know every last detail of the winds in this sea?*"

An instant later, a violent gust of wind smacked Rodolphe in the face…

…and caught the sails of the enemy vessel.

Legul drove his naval ram right into the side of Rodolphe's flagship.

"Looks like we're done here," Legul muttered under his breath as he looked down at the sinking galley, hull gaping with a ram-size hole.

His foe's ship had been wrecked. The others had lost the will to keep going—either fleeing the scene or surrendering on the spot.

"All that's left is locating Rodolphe…"

The ocean below was filled with galley sailors clawing through the ship. It'd be hard for even Legul to pick out the face of a man he hadn't seen in over a decade.

He caught sight of a single boat bursting out from the shadow of the galley. Two oarsmen and one passenger. One face seemed familiar.

"Ditching his subordinates to save himself, huh? And he dares to call himself a *Kelil*."

"Sir Legul, the enemy sailors are requesting aid. What shall we do?"

"Leave them. A sea burial is fitting for sailor pawns. Chase that boat."

After Legul gave his subordinates orders, his expression suddenly soured.

"...Tch. Faster than I thought."

Straight ahead, on the distant horizon, he saw the shadows of two fleets of ships.

"Those are...the flags of two *Kelil*, Emelance and Sandia!"

That's right, Legul agreed wordlessly.

Only the *Kelil* would act in this situation. Of course they were rushing to the aid of their fellow *Kelil* Rodolphe.

—Or not. What they were after was the Rainbow Crown.

"Sir Legul, we have enough power and morale to take on another battle."

"...No, we'll retreat."

Legul knew tragedy had befallen Rodolphe because of his inflated ego.

The other two *Kelil* must have been watching their battle and noticed that Legul's sailing vessel moved deftly. He didn't think he'd lose, but he might take unexpected damage.

"We'll lay siege to the island where Rodolphe has his stronghold while keeping a safe distance from the other fleets. They're obviously not here to lend us a helping hand, but I doubt they'll try and draw blood."

"Understood."

The subordinate signaled the other ships, and Legul's fleet slowly began to leave for other waters.

"A one-sided battle, eh?" Tolcheila observed from their ship hidden in the shadow of an island. Her eyes trailed after Legul leaving the aftermath. "Legul is the real deal."

"He certainly does know how to handle a ship. Goodness, that was a surprise."

Voras nodded in admiration. Even though a fellow *Kelil* was just soundly defeated, it didn't seem like it affected him.

"So, Voras, what do you think will happen next?"

"They will be in a deadlock for some time, I presume," he answered. "I do not know what has become of Rodolphe, but I imagine he escaped. That man is rather persistent, after all. I suppose he will hole up in his manor for the time being."

"But he'll starve to death if he's surrounded. Rodolphe will have nowhere to turn. If Legul sends his crew ashore to torture him, he may break long before that."

"There is no fear of that happening. After all, the *Kelil* closing in at the end of the battle would then turn their weapons against Legul."

"You mean Emelance and Sandia? It was sly of them to make an appearance once the battle had already been decided."

Tolcheila and Voras had watched as the two fleets had entered Rodolphe and Legul's battle. Staying out of sight had been the right choice for the princess and her temporary keeper.

"Legul's forces are undeniably powerful—when they're among ships and seas. But for ground warfare and marching directly into the manor, they're not much stronger than your average soldiers," Voras remarked.

"I see; so it is the ocean that gives them strength. If those two *Kelil* take one step on the island, Legul's soldiers will put knives in *their* backs. They can't be careless. It's a deadlock. Will Rodolphe accept aid or surrender?"

Voras shook his head. "I very much doubt it. Now that he has been captivated by the Rainbow Crown, he will never agree to relinquish it."

"Maybe the other two will conspire to attack Rodolphe?"

"That would be difficult. They aren't allies but rivals, both aiming for the Rainbow Crown. If they took the time to negotiate, the two could temporarily join forces, but Legul will call reinforcements to the stronghold beforehand."

"Hmm, I see. So the stalemate will last until Legul requests extra aid. Whether or not Rodolphe hides away in his manor or the two *Kelil* look for their chance to strike, we must make a move before then."

Tolcheila looked stunned but hated herself for it.

"Everything happened *just as he said*."

"Indeed it has."

Voras's gentle demeanor was touched by fear.

"He's a fearsome fellow—that Prince Wein."

Rodolphe was going to carry the Rainbow Crown away from the island.

Days had passed since his naval fleet had sunk into the sea. With nowhere else to turn—unable to even lock himself away in his manor—this had been his last resort.

"Sir Rodolphe, we're ready."

"Right…"

He was going to take an emergency route that he'd prepared in case anything went awry. It was a cave that led to the ocean. A small escape boat bobbed in the waters before him.

This would be his ticket out.

"Damn Legul… I won't forget this…!" Rodolphe muttered as he got in the boat.

It was humiliating. He'd lost years of accumulated military power and, essentially, his title. His situation looked bleak now that his fortune was all but lost.

The one thing that kept him from losing all hope was the precious Rainbow Crown in the box he was holding.

With this, I can start over… even if I lose everything else.

He gripped the box tightly. This Rainbow Crown roused Rodolphe's heart, although he had nothing. It acted as a final lifeline.

"Let us get going."

The boat set off slowly.

The cave led to the southwest sector of the island. The waters here were shallow, and any large vessel heavy enough to sink deep in the water was unable to pass. There were numerous reefs, and any ship that tried to enter unawares was almost guaranteed to run aground. Even Legul and the two *Kelil* couldn't approach it. Attempting to sail through these waters on a cloudy, starless night was basically suicide.

And so that was the path Rodolphe would take.

I know this place like the back of my hand. So do my men. Even if no stars are out, we'll be able to navigate the reef with our experience and the lighthouse.

They emerged from the cave and entered the reef as he'd expected, passing through without incident. They would have to stay alert and watch out for enemy patrols. How could the group avoid them?

Even a blockade has limits. If we can weave between the guards and break through—

Rodolphe's mind was racing.

"…Hmm?"

Something about the sight before him felt off.

"What…?"

It was strange. Everything was going according to plan, but something didn't feel right. He wasn't sure why, but his seafaring experience was setting off alarm bells in his head.

Rodolphe looked around him. The inky ocean. A cloudy sky. The glow of the lighthouse visible from the other side of the sea. Everything passed through his field of vision—until he noticed the thing he dreaded.

"Stop the boat! Now!" he barked.

The sailor controlling the boat jolted.

A moment later, something rocked the boat.

"GWAGH—?!"

Almost everyone in the boat was launched off, plummeting straight into the sea. Rodolphe clung to the vessel, clutching the box containing the Rainbow Crown for dear life.

Then he saw that the boat was in the air, a jagged rock piercing through the floorboards.

"A reef?! Why is that here?!" one of the sailors cried out in anguish.

They'd crossed these waters more times than they could count. The seafarers all swore the reef hadn't been there before.

"It's the lighthouse…"

Rodolphe knew the answer, and his voice trembled. He gazed upon the light beyond the darkness. "There's something different about the light coming from the lighthouse…!"

His sailor subordinates turned toward it, realizing what their master said was true. The light was not in its usual location.

The lighthouse was a crucial compass that allowed safe passage through the darkness. It was not something those who often traveled these waters would ever doubt. And it was the reason they had run aground.

There was the question of whether this was all part of someone's plan.

A midsize ship soundlessly crept up before them in the night. He knew the person standing at its edge.

"Master…Felite…?!"

"It's been a while, Rodolphe."

Felite Zarif faced the stunned man and offered a small smile.

"We don't have enough people," Wein started as he explained his plan. "I highly doubt Rodolphe will hand over the Rainbow Crown if we visit him, and we don't have the military power to rip it from his hands. —So we'll spread rumors throughout all of Patura that he has it."

He paused, then went on.

"Once Legul hears of this, he'll confirm whether the rumors are true. After all, if Rodolphe doesn't have the crown or know where it is, Legul will have to start from square one."

"Even if Legul dispatches one of his subordinates with the task, he'll have to shoulder the risk that they might keep the Rainbow Crown for themselves. Legul will take his fleet and go straight to him himself," Felite replied. "But what if Legul defeats Rodolphe and takes the crown?"

"We'd have another *Kelil* cut in," Wein replied. "Rodolphe has been one for a long time, right? If even he stole the crown, there had to be at least two or three others with the same goal."

Wein motioned to one of the documents in his hand. It came from the library and contained all sorts on information on the *Kelil*.

"Based on these papers, Emelance, Sandia, and Corvino seem to have their own plans in mind. Let's have them fight for the Rainbow Crown and create a deadlock."

"'Create a deadlock'…? And how would we do that?" Felite asked.

"We'll let Rodolphe escape. With the crown." Wein pointed to another sheet of paper. "There's a reef in the southwest part of the island where Rodolphe has his stronghold. Once his island is surrounded, I imagine he'll try to escape from there under the cover of night. That's where we'll catch him. Even if he dies in the battle or gets assassinated, someone else will try to escape from these islands with the treasure. That is, if the magic of the Rainbow Crown is the real deal."

"…Indeed. Now that it is in his possession, I cannot easily imagine Rodolphe relinquishing it to anyone, even at the cost of his life. If there is a path of escape, he will take it. Will we be able to catch him? The waters are dangerous at night. Rodolphe is confident in his ability to navigate them with his crew."

"That's why we're going to make them run ashore. We'll fake the location of their lighthouse."

"What…?"

Disguise the lighthouse?

Felite had never entertained such an idea before. He immediately unfurled the sea chart before them. After confirming the positions of the surrounding islands and lighthouses, he understood what the prince was suggesting. This would probably work.

"It'll likely disorient Legul and the *Kelil*'s patrol boats, too. All we have to do is sneak past the guards into the reef, capture Rodolphe, and secretly make our escape. The next leader of Patura should be able to pull that off in his sleep. Right?"

"You make it sound so easy…but I will do it."

They had a lot to do. It was going to be a dangerous bridge to cross. Even so, Felite felt Wein's plot would be more effective than his own plan to win over each *Kelil* individually.

"Um…I have a question." Apis raised her hand. "I believe we have connections on each island that we can contact to spread rumors. However, you may need the proper assistance and materials if you wish to do something to the lighthouse…"

"That's true. We'll need to get in touch with one of the *Kelil*. Aside from mobilizing fleets, we should be able to work something out if they're willing to lend us supplies and people. We can compensate them later."

"Is there a *Kelil* we can trust? It'll be reckless to decide based on the information in these documents. I mean, even Sir Rodolphe betrayed us for the Rainbow Crown," Felite added.

"That's what the rumors are for."

Apis cocked her head in confusion.

Felite seemed to understand. "You're planning on testing their loyalty by seeing whether they'll join the fray…?!"

Wein nodded. "There will be those who will plan to take Patura for themselves upon hearing the rumors. And there will be those who offer no reaction—because they have no ambitions, no courage, or no interest. I'll have the latter convinced in no time."

He wasn't bluffing. Wein sounded certain that he could make this a reality.

"At the top of my list," Wein continued, "is Voras, the guy that's accommodating Princess Tolcheila. If he doesn't plan on joining the fray, we can talk. I'd better see him in person." He looked at Felite. "What do you think? From your documents, this is the best I could come up with."

"…To be honest, there is a part of me that thinks this is impossible to pull off. But I'm amazed by your ideas. To think you'd be able to concoct this plan from these papers... If we can pull this off, it will be extremely satisfying."

"You've got a real sinister flair." Wein held out his hand to Felite. "Come on. Let's be bad wolves together."

I've heard the rumors, but this is something else...

Felite had never imagined the prince would be able to formulate such a plan just by skimming some papers. Even he was struck with awe.

Wein, of course, had proposed more than one plot—and he'd also calculated myriad other scenarios. One could say the prince was bound to come across a winning idea after considering so many, but the truth was that he'd suggested the other plans only to put Felite and Apis at ease. From the start, he'd known this would be the best of all of them.

I thought we both believed history and knowledge were priceless. I wasn't wrong, but he equips himself with this knowledge far better than I've managed to do!

Felite glanced next to him, eyeing Wein and Ninym, who were accompanying him aboard the ship. The prince was indeed the Dragon of the North. He was more dependable than one hundred soldiers. Maybe even one thousand of his best men.

Even though everything is going to plan, he expresses no joy, remaining stoically calm... It's as if he expected this outcome, Felite thought.

Wein was caught up in his head, too. *Urp. I shouldn't have come. I'm going to throw up if this ship doesn't stop rocking.* He was trying his best to keep a straight face.

Not that Felite could read his mind.

"—Surrender, Rodolphe," Felite whispered to the man. "Your ship can no longer make the journey. Even if you struggle, there is no escaping here. If you surrender peacefully, we promise to spare the lives of both you and your crew."

It was a magnanimous decision; Rodolphe had stolen the Rainbow Crown, a symbol of authority. No one would blame Felite if he went on a murderous rampage.

The crew surrounding Rodolphe understood this. They knew they were at an extreme disadvantage. They looked at each other in mutual agreement before nervously turning to Rodolphe.

"........." Rodolphe looked up at Felite, then down at the box in his arms. If he surrendered, he'd lose the Rainbow Crown. His face twisted bitterly.

"...I suppose there's no other way. Apis," said Felite, realizing they were getting nowhere.

"Right."

Led by Apis, a crew of sailors, each armed with a sword, boarded Rodolphe's boat.

"Sir Rodolphe, please hand it over," Apis said, pointing the tip of her sword at him.

He had betrayed her. If he resisted, she would kill him.

"...You're telling me to return this?"

Felite nodded. "Yes. The Rainbow Crown isn't yours."

"But...!"

"You were the one who taught me how to sail. I don't wish to taint that memory with blood."

Felite was pleading with Rodolphe not to make him raise his sword. To him, the *Kelil* were close aides who had supported his father. And it wasn't just Rodolphe. Every person on Rodolphe's ship was worthy of honor. Felite didn't want to harm them if he could help it.

"......"

As if Felite had gotten through to him, Rodolphe slowly passed the box to Apis, hands trembling after a long period of agonizing deliberation.

"...You've made the right choice." Felite looked at the box in Apis's hands, letting out a sigh of relief. "Please see them safely onto the ship. We'll be departing soon."

His own sailors and the opposing crew clambered aboard. Just to be safe, Rodolphe's gang was tied up with rope.

Apis presented the box to Felite. "Please check its contents, Master Felite."

She snapped open the box. Light sprang forth from the darkness. Felite instinctively narrowed his eyes. Within the box was a multicolored seashell that emitted a mysterious shine.

"...It's real."

They had recovered the symbol of authority. Their mission was accomplished, but Felite felt no joy. In fact, it pained him to gaze at the Rainbow Crown.

"Apis, lock that box away in the ship's hold and place it under strict security."

"Understood." She turned away on her heel, taking the treasure with her.

"—Ah, I knew it. I can't take it."

Something blurred in the corner of Felite's vision. Before he even had the chance to perceive it, Rodolphe had seized the sword of a nearby sailor and was racing toward Apis.

"Apis!" Felite screamed, shoving her out of the way.

"The Rainbow Crown's mine!" Rodolphe rushed in with beast-like ferocity.

"Forgive me, Rodolphe...!"

A moment passed. Felite's unsheathed blade had sliced cleanly across Rodolphe's body.

"Gah—?!" The man spewed blood, crumpling to his knees.

Felite's brow creased with regret, but before he could fully process his actions, he heard another cry.

"Th-the box!"

Felite witnessed the case sliding across the deck. It must have fallen out of Apis's arms when he'd pushed her. It inched over the edge, about to fall into the ocean—

"—Hup!" Wein skidded over, leaning over the ship, just narrowly grabbing the box.

"Your Highness!"

"Prince Wein!"

"Don't congratulate me yet! Ninym! Help me out! I'm about to fall along with it."

Krck. Just as Wein called for backup, the lid of the box snapped off its hinges.

"Ah."

The Rainbow Crown plunged below the ship. It sounded like something had shattered.

"".........""

Everyone on the ship held their breath. Ninym took a step forward and quietly checked the waters below. There she saw Rodolphe's ship, which had previously run aground.

"I don't know how to say this," Ninym spoke up nervously, gaping at the rainbow shards sprayed all over the deck. "I apologize for being the bearer of bad news—but the Rainbow Crown is destroyed."

Wein and Felite looked at each other.

Chapter 4 | The Loss of Legends

A lavish guest room in Voras's mansion housed Wein and Ninym, faces clouded over.

"About what Felite said…" Wein broke the silence. "Didn't he need the Rainbow Crown because he couldn't unify Patura on his own?"

"Uh-huh."

"And now that treasure is in pieces."

"Uh-huh."

"…What do you think of our situation?"

Ninym offered a small nod. "I'd say it's checkmate."

"RIIIIIIIGHT?!" Wein clawed at his head with his hands.

The group had arrived at Voras's place earlier that morning. The ship's crew had been placed under a gag order. They all needed some time to rest, but it wouldn't be long before Voras found out. After all, most of the sailors were originally on loan from the man himself.

If they didn't do something, the truth was going to reach all corners of Patura.

"If that happens, Legul will win."

At present, Legul had the strongest naval force in these parts. Wein's group needed to join hands with the islands' leaders to defeat him, but now they'd lost their leverage.

"I wonder what we should do…" Ninym crossed her arms.

The symbol was in fragments. She thought they could find a

suitable replacement, but she hadn't been able to think of anything so far that could fill such a role.

"Felite's been holed up in his room, huh...? I'm guessing he's devastated."

"But we cannot afford to waste our time here. We must keep in mind that we may have to wash our hands of this and abandon them."

"Yeah. I guess."

Wein was an outsider. The influence of his delegation was limited since they had no roots here, but it also meant they could make a quick escape if necessary.

"But Legul might have already figured out my identity... And if he wins, our relationship will Patura will be—" Wein began.

"The North and South have never really interacted with one another. We can leave them to figure out their own mess by themselves if necessary."

Ninym was right, but Wein found himself feeling a little sympathetic. Besides...it wasn't as if Wein didn't have a plan to turn things around.

"Prince Wein! You've returned!"

The doors swung open to reveal Tolcheila. She had gotten back from her naval observations and now looked at him with the biggest smile.

"I apologize that I could not be there to greet you," she chattered. "I couldn't pull myself away from assisting with the feast to celebrate your victory. You know, I expected no less of you, Prince Wein! Predicting the shifting tides of battle is nothing short of incredible! I can now see how you defeated my fath— Hmm?"

Tolcheila stopped midsentence, noticing Wein's tense expression.

"Why do you look so down? Is there a problem? You have the Rainbow Crown, don't you?"

"Yes, well, yeah, we do." Wein kind of nodded.

Word of its demolition hadn't yet reached her ears, it seemed.

"In that case, all is well. Oh yes, where is Sir Felite?"

Ninym was the one to answer. "Sir Felite informed us that he has much to consider and retired to his room. He may…be there for quite some time."

"I see. Well, I suppose it's only natural, given recent events," she responded, having no clue about his wretched situation. "If there's extra time before our next plan, that's perfect. There is something I wish to discuss with you, Prince Wein. I imagine you must be exhausted, but might I have a moment of your time?"

Something to discuss? Wein nodded, wondering what it could possibly be.

"You put in a good word for us with Sir Voras, after all. I don't mind."

Upon confirming that Voras hadn't jumped at the rumors of Rodolphe possessing the Rainbow Crown, Wein had contacted the man, requesting the *Kelil*'s support. Tolcheila had really backed him up there.

"Then let's go. I've already prepared the venue."

"Understood. Will we be conversing in your room, Princess Tolcheila?"

She shook her head, beaming at him.

"No. We're going to the beach."

Deep blue sea. White clouds. Sand baking under the sun.

Tolcheila soaked it all up. "Perfect weather for a private chat!"

"'A private chat'…?"

"Why do you appear so puzzled, Prince Wein? Look around us. There is no one else on this beach. Better here than in a room with hidden witnesses."

"I can agree, but I do have one question."

"What might that be?"

"Why are we dressed like this?"

Wein and Tolcheila were in swimsuits.

"We told the others that you were relaxing by the beach. Wouldn't it be strange if we weren't in swimsuits?"

Would it really be that strange? Wein had his suspicions, but Tolcheila drew close to him, trying to dispel those feelings.

"Besides, Prince Wein, don't you have anything to say about my figure?"

Wein looked her outfit up and down. "How flat."

"Princess kick!"

She booted him.

"You don't understand! Not in the least! My body is still growing! One day, I shall mature! Listen well. My figure is not childish—it's simply under construction! An unpolished gem of possibilities! My body invented the word 'precious'! I shall grant you one more chance to redeem yourself!"

"How small."

"Princess punch!"

She landed her blow.

"U-um…" called out a nervous voice.

"M-may I change back into my normal clothes…?" Ninym asked, covering up her body with a long strip of cloth.

She was hunched in on herself, red up to the tips of her ears, which was rare for her.

"What's with that cloth? Toss the boorish thing. Even my own servants are proudly wearing swimsuits of their own."

As Tolcheila had stated, they all stood at attention nearby in their own swimwear.

Ninym refused to give it up. "Ah, well, it's just… To expose myself in public is…"

"Hmm? Ah, yes, it always snows in Natra. I suppose your people don't show their skin, aside from baths, much less in front of one's lord."

"Y-yes. And so…"

"Well, this is the perfect opportunity to get used to it! Strip!"

Ninym wondered when this girl would ever quit.

"Ah, please wait, Princess Tolcheila."

It was here that Wein finally stepped in.

"Ninym acts as my guard. She needs to be prepared to deal with emergencies."

"Y-yes," the aide squeaked out. "So…"

"But I love seeing her out of her element! Nice one!"

"You *do* understand, Prince Wein!" Tolcheila squealed.

One day, Ninym was going to kill them both.

"Come! Fight us no longer!"

"Hold on, wai—!"

The other servants tore away her cloth, revealing pale skin and a black bathing suit.

"Oh my! It suits you well, I must admit. Not that you can best me!"

Tolcheila sounded pleased, but Ninym was in no mood to hear it. Her alabaster skin was tinged crimson as she hugged herself in an effort to conceal her figure.

"What embarrasses you? Ever heard 'all who are easy on the eye live life dignified'? There is no need for you to cower in shame," the princess urged. "Face the sun and thrust out your chest."

Ninym retreated to her inner monologue, where she could chew Tolcheila out. As she prepared for the fight to shield her body, Ninym noticed Wein staring at her.

His gaze was gentle. Even as she was about to explode from embarrassment, he was like the glassy surface of a windless sea.

Suddenly, she felt a flash of anger. How could he be so calm while she was having a mini heart attack?

Desperate to turn the attention to anything else, she decided to stir his calm waters with some wind.

She turned on him. "...Why don't you say something?"

Just saying the words made her feel faint. What was this? Why was she pouting for attention—hiding her hands behind her and averting her gaze? Wasn't she ready to engage in full-out war?

"Um, just forget it..." Ninym tried to backtrack, but she couldn't seem to find any words to say.

Wein finally answered. "It looks great on you, Ninym."

"―――"

Her heart nearly exploded. She found it impossible to look directly at him. She certainly didn't want to imagine what her own face looked like either. But she knew that her tense expression had slackened into a smile. If she turned away now, it would be the same as admitting defeat. Not that this was a competition or anything!

—Agh, enough!

The sun was to blame. And the ocean and the sand. Yeah. That was it.

Ninym was glad Wein and Tolcheila were the only ones around. If her friends from her school days had seen her, she could only imagine what a field day they would have had.

Telling herself there was always a silver lining, she willed her pounding heart to be still.

"—Ack?!"

"Something wrong, Princess Lowellmina?"

"I feel like I'm somehow missing out on something very important…! Something to give me joke material for the next ten years!"

"Now I'm certain you've caught a cold, Your Highness…"

"N-no! I'm perfectly healthy! Hey! Why are you calling the physician?! There is no need! Ah! Wait! Don't make me take that bitter medicine— *Blergh?!*"

"Let us get to the subject at hand," Tolcheila said to get things started.

Ninym had calmed down, resuming her role as Wein's aide with slightly blushing cheeks.

The princess sprawled out on a bed woven from tree bark. "While you were taking care of your own business, I looked into the situation myself. I researched Legul's background and confirmed something fascinating."

"What might that be?"

"He's backed by Vanhelio."

Even Wein was surprised.

Vanhelio was a nation in the southwestern part of the continent, comparable to the Northern nation of Soljest for two reasons.

It had about the same amount of military power, and Vanhelio had Steel as a Holy Elite, just as Soljest had King Gruyere.

"You mean the Holy Elite Steel Lozzo…Vanhelio's 'Artist Duke'?"

Wein had met Steel during the Festival of the Spirit. His impression was that he wished to be nowhere near the man.

"I cannot say whether Steel has a direct connection to Legul, but there's no question that he has Vanhelio's support, and they are the ones maintaining his fleet. Can you guess, Prince Wein, what Vanhelio is after and why they're backing Legul?"

Certainly not out of pity for the banished son. Legul must have offered something of equal benefit.

""To establish Patura as a bridgehead and invade the Empire.""

Wein and Tolcheila's voices overlapped perfectly.

"Seems we've both come to the same conclusion," she said.

"It is the only plausible one. Though Patura leans slightly to the West, it's remained neutral. If it aligns with that part of the continent, it will disrupt the power balance in the South."

"The islanders are unlikely to put up much of a fight. After all, they have bad blood with the Empire."

The Empire had launched many attempts to colonize Patura. The Zarif had established nonaggressive defense policies, favoring neither East nor West, but Patura viewed the Empire as a threat to its freedom.

"...If the Empire were stable, the West wouldn't stand a chance, even with the Patura navy on its side. Right?" Wein asked.

"Correct. However, that's not the case right now. The Imperial Princes are still fighting for the throne. If Steel and Legul's plan succeeds, they can infiltrate places deep within the Empire."

Wein agreed with this assessment. In fact, he thought it was extremely likely.

"Well, now that that's out of the way, we can continue our talk in secret." Tolcheila's lips spread into a big smile. "So, what say we *kill Felite and join Legul*?"

"_____"

It felt like an icy wind was whipping across the baked beach.

Wein and Tolcheila looked into each other's eyes. The tension was palpable.

"Princess Tolcheila, I'm assuming I may take your words at face value?"

"Indeed. I'm inviting you to abandon the Empire and join the West."

She said this as if it were nothing.

Ninym and Tolcheila's servants scanned the area. They couldn't afford to have anyone overhear this conversation.

No one else was on the empty beach. That was why Tolcheila had chosen this venue.

"I know Natra needed the Empire's protection until just a few years ago. But the kingdom's circumstances have changed," she explained. "You took the gold mine from Marden, won a war against Cavarin, annexed the former Marden territory, and formed friendly alliances with Soljest and Delunio. Natra isn't a small nation anymore. Anyone can see now that it's not to be underestimated."

"I must say it's embarrassing to hear you speak so highly of us." Wein shrugged in jest, but his eyes didn't seem to smile.

"I would not be too excited. I'm saying Natra's opportunistic days of sitting on the fence are over." Tolcheila pressed on. "You have an alliance with an Eastern nation and have formed friendships with two Western ones. This would be fine in a peaceful world, but we're locked in war. Inevitably, you'll make a choice between East and West one day."

Her statement was no exaggeration. Wein had been considering this himself. In fact, it seemed the day of reckoning was not far off.

"As the princess of Soljest, I propose you choose the West. I'm aware of your obligation to the Empire, but I also know that it's caught up in its own mess. Do you have any reason to remain on that sinking ship, Prince Wein? No. If you joined forces with my father and started an invasion from Patura, I believe you could rip your fangs through the Empire's throat."

Tolcheila paused for a moment. She stared intensely at Wein, gauging his reaction. It was rather charming, and Wein smiled before answering.

"I have two things to say to you, Princess Tolcheila."

"Let us hear it." Tolcheila nodded.

"I studied in the Empire on a prior occasion. Taking my experiences into account, I must say you're being too optimistic if you think you can take down the Empire."

"You mean they still have influence despite looking like a sorry mess?"

"There is proof of it. After all, it's still kicking. There are many who refuse to get involved in the fight for power between the bureaucrats and the princes. Instead, they wait quietly in the shadows and focus their energies on keeping the nation alive. If the West attacked, they would unite and rise up."

"Hmm…"

Tolcheila's expression said she was reluctant to accept this. Since she'd never set foot in the Empire, she must have found it hard to believe it could have such people while exhausting its resources in the fight over succession.

Wein, however, knew this all too well. He had seen the Empire with his own two eyes. Their dignitaries were the genuine article. The country was not to be taken lightly because of its current situation.

"…Very well. Forget my reckless plan and forgive me for acting in my own self-interest. I just wanted to see you and my father side by side on the battlefield."

"I am not much help when it comes to battle."

"Don't say that. Isn't it romantic for my husband to fight alongside my father?"

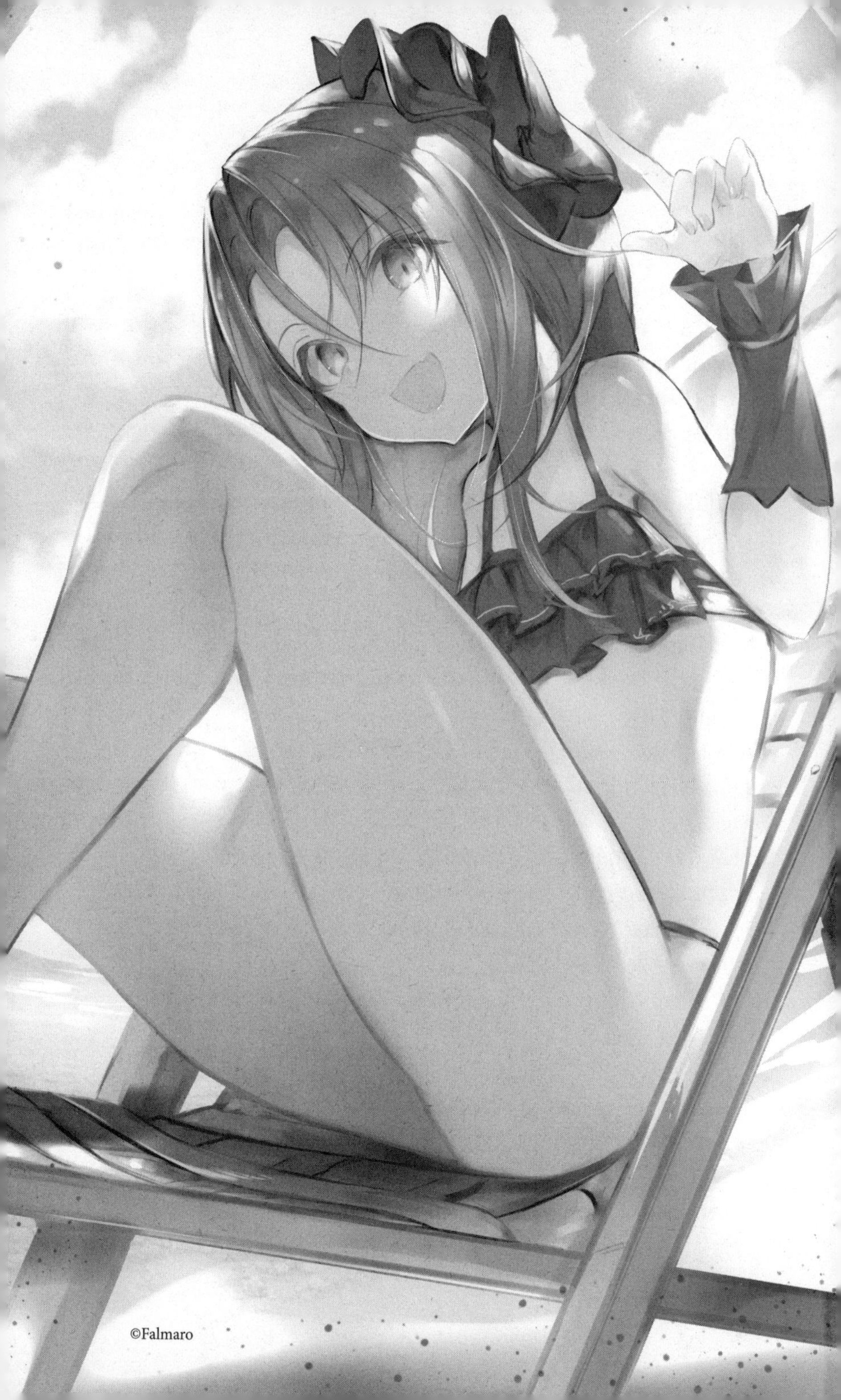
©Falmaro

"Well, I'm afraid I don't know much about that. Hold up—Husband?"

"Yes. If you plan to attack the East with my father, we will need to secure an alliance through marriage. Ah, but worry not. I shall permit mistresses." Tolcheila gave a pointed glance at Ninym.

The aide averted her gaze with an indescribable look on her face.

She continued. "Ah, well, let's put the matter aside for now. In any case, are you sure you don't want to join Legul? After all, blood would only be spilled in the Empire and Vanhelio. Natra can remain uninvolved, but I imagine the Empire might try to form an alliance with you, bringing you an offer you can't resist, if things get messy in the South."

"That's related to another point of discussion." Wein's tone dropped. "I wish to confirm this ahead of time: How exactly do you plan to from a partnership between me and Legul?"

"Just bring him Felite's head and the Rainbow Crown. I imagine someone working with Vanhelio will do their best to accommodate the princess of Soljest."

"Ah… Yes, well, I suppose that's true."

"Why so cagey? Does something worry you?"

Wein and Ninym exchanged looks. She nodded, departing the scene. Tolcheila tilted her head.

"I hate to say this, but the Rainbow Crown…broke when we tried to recover it."

"Excuse me?" Tolcheila blinked at him. She sat silent for a moment before nervously asking for more information. "Y-you must mean it got a little chipped around the edges, right…?"

"It's probably best that I show you…"

Just then, Ninym returned, holding some fruits. She took out a juicy one—and crushed it to bits right in front of Tolcheila.

"Like that."

"Eeeeeeeep?!" Tolcheila shrieked. "What happened?! Didn't you say you brought it back?!"

"We did bring it back. In pieces."

"Are you saying you can't put it back together?!"

"We gathered up as many fragments as we could, but I suppose Legul wouldn't want it that way, huh?"

"He'd obviously go mad and cut off every head in sight, including yours and mine——!"

Wein winced. He could see it.

"I—I can't believe this is happening…! Oh no! If it's revealed that I was part of this, our diplomatic relations with Vanhelio could be in jeopardy…! I must do everything in my power to ensure my involvement is never made known!"

"I'm so sorry."

"How dare you muster an empty apology with a straight face…?!" Tolcheila held her head in her hands and glared at Wein. "So what do *you* plan on doing, Prince Wein?! Felite doesn't stand a chance without the Rainbow Crown!"

"Regardless of his chances, we will not get anywhere if Sir Felite refuses to leave his room, to say the very least. I'd like him to join us as soon as possible, but—"

Just then, Wein spotted a human shadow creeping toward them from the heart of the island. It was Felite's servant Apis.

"Pardon me," Apis said, kneeling before them. "Master Felite wishes to speak with Prince Wein. My apologies, but I ask that you make your way to his room."

"Tell him I'll be right there."

Wein turned to Ninym, whispering in her ear.

"It looks like things might move along after all."

Before him was the box that held the broken bits of the Rainbow Crown. Felite couldn't rip his eyes away from it as he thought back to his past.

It was a memory he'd revisited time and time again.

Mighty father. Kind mother. An older brother he revered so much.

A picture-perfect, happy family torn apart twelve years prior.

"Why won't anyone obey me?!"

The memory always began with his brother's screams.

His brother was a natural genius—a miracle child who had understood the subtleties of the sea since the day of his birth. All were confident he would pave a golden path to their future.

However, his talent gradually created friction with those around him.

"Everyone else is garbage compared to me! Why won't they recognize me for me? Just look at me! I'm the one who should be standing above you all!"

He was in his own little world. To normal people, his emotional complexity was invisible, unconveyable, incomprehensible, and it frustrated him to live this way. He found fault with everyone and spun out of control—going from "child prodigy" to "dissenter." Admiration turned to scorn.

Felite always wondered if their futures would have been different if he'd been able to rescue even the smallest fragment of his brother's heart back then.

The memory offered no answer.

There had been a terrible storm that day.

"Stop it, Legul!" shrieked their mother, sounding heartbroken.

As wind raged and rain poured, Felite raced down the hallway.

"What do you plan on doing by taking that with you?!"

"Isn't it obvious?! I'll get everyone to recognize my true worth!"

A fight between mother and son. Her words fell on deaf ears.

Panic rattled Felite's entire body as he launched himself off the ground to find them.

"I'm worth more than anyone, but no one can see that! Then I've got no choice but to make them understand with the power of this treasure!"

"Legul, you mustn't be misled! Even without it, you will be accepted by all! Just bear it a while longer…!"

"I'm sick of waiting! If you're going to get in my way, I won't be nice, Mother!"

"Legul!"

Thunder clapped. The world flooded with white.

Felite slid into the room where he'd heard the voices.

"_____"

He froze in place. Before him were his collapsed mother and his stone-still brother. Blood pumped out from his mother's body, and there was a blood-soaked blade on the ground nearby.

In his brother's raised hand shone the ominous gleam of the Rainbow Crown.

"Yes… Now everything is mine."

Felite stared as his brother raised the treasure without so much as a second glance at their fallen mother.

This is the moment our paths as siblings diverged—

The guards rushed in to capture his brother. Their father, utterly despondent from the loss of his wife, banished him. Alois couldn't bring himself to execute his own child, though Legul had murdered his wife.

Legul, however, took no notice of his father's anguish.

"I'll be back! I guarantee I'll return to this land once more! The Rainbow Crown is mine!"

With that last curse, Legul disappeared from Patura. Felite had the distinct sense that they would clash again in the future.

Twelve years later, his brother was keeping his promise. Their broken paths met at a final crossroad, and it had come time for one to end.

And whose path would be cut off—his brother's or his own?

"Master Felite, I've brought Prince Wein."

The voice from the other side of the door roused Felite from his sea of memories.

"Come in."

Apis entered the room with Wein and Ninym.

"I apologize for calling you here, Prince Wein."

"No problem at all," Wein replied.

Felite looked at him and tilted his head. "Oh... Did you get some sun?"

"We were just outside."

"The weather is nice. Not even a single gust of wind. It's rare for us to have a chance to sunbathe at this time of year."

He'd been too caught up in his own thoughts to notice. The rays streaked through the windows. If not for their situation, he would have been out there enjoying the sunshine himself.

"It looks like you've been brooding. Is it because we lost the Rainbow Crown?" Wein asked as he took a seat.

Felite shook his head. "No, I was just recalling an unpleasant memory. The loss of the Rainbow Crown will cause issues in the future, but I'm actually—"

"Relieved?"

"...You can tell?"

"Well, I sort of figured out that you hated it, Sir Felite."

Wein had apparently seen right through him. Felite wasn't even surprised anymore, seeing that the prince could pick up so much from so little.

"I only saw the article before it fell into the boat, but…I definitely see how its shine might tempt people."

"Yes. One might say it's evil incarnate. There are even records of the blood-soaked history that followed the Zarif for pursuing the Rainbow Crown."

"Does that light absorb people's life force?"

"Maybe… I have wished for its destruction for many years. Even so, it happened so quickly that I needed some time to settle my beating heart." Felite chuckled sardonically. "Of course, since we've lost a tool vital to the broader picture, I realize I can't afford to be happy. Therefore, I wish for you to lend me your wisdom once more, Prince Wein."

"You don't plan on giving up?"

"Not in the least," Felite declared. He seemed indomitable—now that he was free from being forced to use the Rainbow Crown that he so loathed.

"All right. In that case, I have one plan up my sleeve. However, Sir Felite, you'll need to have resolve and acting skills."

"That suits me just fine."

Wein grinned. "First, let's bring all the *Kelil* here as soon as possible."

Legul couldn't hide his irritation.

Rodolphe had hidden himself away on land, surrounded by Legul and two *Kelil*—Emelance and Sandia. They bared their fangs over the Rainbow Crown and created a sort of power equilibrium, but

Legul destroyed that delicate balance when he called an additional fleet from the central island.

As he sent a portion of his soldiers on land to raid Rodolphe's mansion, Legul used his main army and reinforcements to keep Emelance and Sandia in check. In the end, they were both pressured to retreat.

Finally, Legul's faction gained control of Rodolphe's estate.

"Where the hell is that damn man…?!"

Neither the Rainbow Crown nor Rodolphe was to be found. According to apprehended eyewitnesses, Rodolphe had disappeared shortly after he had been surrounded by the three fleets, leaving behind his subordinates. They weren't about to put up a fight, but they couldn't seem to agree about whom they wanted to surrender to, and Legul had launched his attack before they could come to a decision.

After a bit of investigating, he learned there was a secret pathway from the mansion that led to the reefs. There was no question Rodolphe had used this path to escape. His destination, however, was unknown.

Did Rodolphe ask another Kelil for help…? No. If he did that, the Rainbow Crown would be stolen from him. Without an army or money, there's no way he can make a comeback on his own.

Legul had no clue where Rodolphe was. It wasn't like he was going to give up, though.

I'll get my hands on the Rainbow Crown…and show that I'm the ruler of the seas!

Legul might once have been praised as a genius, but even he didn't have divine insight. He had no way of knowing that Rodolphe was already dead and Felite was in possession of the Rainbow Crown. Most of all, he was unaware the Rainbow Crown had been smashed to pieces.

And so Legul was fired up, continuing to search for signs of Rodolphe.

During all this, he never realized that his younger brother Felite was making a difficult decision behind closed doors.

Wein and Felite dove headfirst into contacting the *Kelil* and worked behind the scenes in secrecy.

The message was a summons. The *Kelil* each reacted to it differently, but in the end, they complied, at least on the outside, to the appeal above Felite's name. The fact that the specified location was the home of a more senior *Kelil*—Voras—must have kept them in line.

Five of them were gathered in the dim conference room within the Voras estate.

Voras. Emelance. Sandia. Corvino. Edgar. True leaders of the Patura Archipelago.

"My goodness. The winds this year are something, huh?"

"Seriously. We're having warmer weather than usual this spring."

"On my way here, I saw that the rhododendrons were already blooming."

The *Kelil* remained on their guard, probing the true motives of the others while engaging in casual conversation. They were, of course, all *Kelil*. A slip of the tongue wouldn't come so easily.

They were trying to calculate the best opponent and timing to cut each other down. Someone finally spoke up after they verbally paced around each other, sizing up the others.

"…At any rate, I'm rather surprised to see Master Felite at your home, Sir Voras."

It was Sandia. Of all the members, he was the newest, with the biggest ambitions. Proof of this was in the fact that he had traveled to Rodolphe's island in pursuit of the Rainbow Crown.

"After all, I was certain he would be with Rodolphe and the Rainbow Crown."

Aside from Voras, the *Kelil* were unaware that Felite and the treasure had temporarily parted. It was only natural that they would assume the two men would be in the same place.

"...Shouldn't Rodolphe be here, Sir Voras?"

This time it was Emelance, refusing to be outdone by Sandia. His goal was to raise an army to steal the Rainbow Crown.

Voras smiled pleasantly. "He might have made it here if your childish sieges had been even faultier than they were. I don't believe someone who's stolen the Rainbow Crown will be visiting me."

"Ngh..." Emelance looked embarrassed.

Sandia shrugged. "Don't sully our good names by calling it a siege. I simply sent out ships to try and protect Sir Rodolphe from Legul. Not that I can speak for this man."

"Sandia! Just who do you think you are...?!"

Emelance and Sandia glared each other down, but someone spoke up to dampen their mood.

"Well, then, do you mean to say that Rodolphe's whereabouts are unknown?"

The speaker was Edgar, the most senior member besides Voras.

"Oh dear. Doesn't he have the Rainbow Crown?" Corvino followed up.

Voras shook his head. "His whereabouts are no issue... He has died."

Everyone looked at him in shock.

Was he bluffing? No way. This old man handed them valuable information only if it was the truth. But how had this happened? And what about the Rainbow Crown?

"...I'd like to hear an explanation, Sir Voras." Finally, Sandia spoke with a cautious look in his eyes.

Voras once again shook his head. "Unfortunately, that is not my duty."

"Well, then, whose duty is it?"

"The answer is obvious. He's just arrived."

All eyes turned to the entrance of the room.

There stood a single man.

"I thank you for coming."

Felite Zarif. Son of the deceased Alois Zarif.

"Ah, Master Felite. I'm glad to see you are well."

Corvino was the first to bow. The others followed suit, expressing their relief over his good health. It was nothing more than lip service. After all, they'd all known he had been captured and had chosen to do nothing to save him.

Felite was aware of this himself.

"Thank you. I, too, am glad to see you all in good spirits."

...Oh? Edgar hadn't been expecting Felite's response. He'd heard the man had undergone grueling interrogations during his capture. Edgar was waiting for a slew of grievances or sarcastic comments, but Felite looked directly at them without a hint of hate. Such a dignified attitude was admirable.

He's always been a bookworm that I could never get a read on... Edgar thought to himself. *But it looks like he's come here with his heart ready.*

Corvino spoke up. "So, Master Felite. Sir Voras already mentioned Sir Rodolphe's passing..."

"I did it myself."

"———" They didn't know what to say.

Felite didn't seem fazed. "I entrusted the Rainbow Crown to Rodolphe to revolt against Legul, but he conspired to use its power for his own ends. As one with the blood of the Zarif flowing through his veins, I passed down his punishment. Are there any objections?"

The *Kelil* looked at one another.

"We have no objections," Voras offered. "It's only natural that using the Rainbow Crown, our island's greatest treasure, for personal gain is worthy of execution."

"I-indeed. Sir Voras is right."

"...I, too, am in agreement."

Corvino and Edgar voiced their approval. At this rate, it would be difficult for Emelance and Sandia to push back. That didn't mean they would back down, though.

"I...I have no objections to Sir Rodolphe's execution. But, Master Felite, if he perished by your hand, then the Rainbow Crown is...?"

"Right here." Felite raised his hand, and Apis appeared at the entrance with a box. She stood by his side and cracked it open with utmost reverence.

Inside was a shell that shone with a rainbow hue.

"Oh...!"

"This light is...!"

Emelance and Sandia instinctively rose from their seats. Voras and Edgar remained motionless.

Corvino gave it a sideways glance, tilting his head. *Doesn't it look a little dull...?*

He wanted to get up and confirm matters for himself, but it was obvious that doing so was impossible in the current situation.

In any case, the Rainbow Crown was safe.

Corvino was going to get a closer look at it when the meeting was over.

"Well, then, shall we get to the matter at hand?"

Felite refocused the *Kelil*'s attention. He was in perfect health and possessed the Rainbow Crown—prerequisites for guiding them into the main discussion.

"It doesn't even need to be said that Legul has brought disorder to Patura. As my father's successor, I need to eliminate him as soon as possible. To do that, I seek the aid of every *Kelil*."

This time, the *Kelil* looked at Voras. Felite's request was well within their expectations; the question was how Voras, who was protecting Felite, would answer. Whether he decided to join Felite would have an impact on whatever happened next.

However, Voras made no move. He made no effort to observe the others' reactions and sat in silence. This implied distance between Voras and Felite.

Will things work out...? Emelance asked himself.

Voras was unpredictable and expressed no interest in power. If he wasn't going to do anything, someone might snatch the Rainbow Crown from Felite—and the Zarif.

Someone will rip the treasure away from the Zarif. I imagine it will be the Kelil *that win the fight against Legul.* Sandia's mind raced.

Legul was strong. Sandia could tell from the skirmish on Rodolphe's island. However, the man was neither matchless nor immortal. If Sandia could get the other *Kelil* to wear each other down, he could take everything for himself in the end.

The Rainbow Crown and Patura shall be mine. Things are about to get interesting...! Corvino was lost in his daydreams.

If Voras wasn't going to do anything, then Edgar was his next hurdle, but Edgar respected Voras as higher in rank. If Voras wasn't going to react, neither would he.

That meant Corvino's main rivals were Emelance and Sandia. If he could just surprise these two, all the treasure, all the praise, and the Rainbow Crown would be his.

...Do these fools honestly think they can beat Legul? Edgar asked himself.

He thought there were only three people who could never be beaten when it came to seafaring: Voras, Alois, and Legul. Despite being over ten years younger than the other two, Legul had exhibited astonishing potential prior to his banishment. Now that he was a grown man, it was almost impossible to imagine the skill he possessed.

We have a 50 percent chance of winning, even if all the Kelil *work together, but I figured Felite would struggle to unite all of them.*

Voras was inscrutable. He knew it would be hard for Felite to manage this task.

Why hadn't the old man expressed that? What plots was he hiding? No one could ever tell what Voras was thinking.

He's loyal to Master Alois. Voras would never join Legul. But there's no chance Legul will meet his end in the sea. It's looking like it might be an inconclusive ending. Edgar let out a small sigh of resignation.

"I have one more thing that I wish to tell you all."

The eyes of the *Kelil* turned to Felite.

"I've hated the Rainbow Crown since I was a child."

Everyone—other than Voras—seemed really confused, faces slack.

Not even giving them a moment to sort out their thoughts, Felite continued. "Does the Rainbow Crown give its possessor physical strength? Does it allow one to handle one's ship with more skill? Does it calm the wind and waves? It doesn't. It's nothing more than a jewel," he said. "But that simple jewel is a harbinger of death. It has a sordid history that includes Rodolphe."

"W-wait," Emelance stuttered, sensing that something wasn't right.

Felite paid him no mind. "I thought to myself, *This is a curse.*"

The *Kelil* gulped. They'd all had an inkling this might be the case. The Rainbow Crown was a destructive force that drew people in, which was why it had a charm that was nearly impossible to resist.

"I'm certain the Rainbow Crown was a holy gift bestowed upon Malaze by the gods, but now it's soaked in blood—hardly a blessing. Even now, this Rainbow Crown is giving birth to war."

Felite seemed to look right through the *Kelil*. Emelance, Sandia, and Corvino averted their gazes, while Voras and Edgar observed Felite's every movement.

"Before coming here, I made two vows." Felite slowly took the Rainbow Crown from within the box. "That I would defeat my brother and restore peace to Patura."

He raised the treasure before the *Kelil*.

"And..." He paused. "And that I would free the islands from the Rainbow Crown!"

Something smashed on the ground.

It was the final melody of the Rainbow Crown as it was thrown violently against the floor.

The eyes of the *Kelil* widened, multicolored fragments scattering before them.

Felite spoke again. "This is my answer."

"You should consider the secret meeting with the *Kelil* as your big debut."

Felite tilted his head. "My big debut?"

"That's right," Wein said. "Now that Alois is gone, you're next in line, but you were captured before you could officially succeed him. Because of this, your authority has slipped away from you and roused the *Kelil*'s own ambitions. Frankly—they're looking down on you."

"...I can't say I disagree."

Like Legul, the *Kelil* wanted control over Patura. They thought Felite was already out of the picture, which was why they disrespected him so brazenly.

Wein continued. "Even if you ask for their cooperation, getting the *Kelil* to side with you will be tough. That's why you'll have to reassert your position in front of them."

"I understand... That's why we have this, right?"

Felite looked at the item nearby. It was the Rainbow Crown, glued back together with tree resin. It had chips and cracks and had lost most of its former glory—but managed to hold its original shape.

"The *Kelil* will eventually find out about the Rainbow Crown. Before they do, I will obliterate it in front of them... I honestly can't say I ever imagined I would see it broken a second time."

If this worked, the *Kelil* would lose their nerve. Nothing could cause more of an impact.

"When they see this symbol of power in smithereens, they're going to be possessed with confusion, rage, despair, shock... We're going to use that to our advantage and persuade them. That's the way we fight." Wein stopped for a beat. "Can you do it, Felite?"

Felite's eyes widened in surprise.

He smiled at the prince. "Let's do it, Wein."

"Wh-what are you doing?!" Emelance shouted first.

"Agh! No...!" Corvino dropped to his knees to collect the pieces by his feet.

"Do you understand what you've done?!" Sandia exclaimed, jumping from his chair.

It worked, Felite thought.

They'd gone through the pains of adjusting the smallest of details to prevent the group from detecting any previous damage sustained by the Rainbow Crown: the positions of Felite and the *Kelil*, the angle at which they viewed the spectacle, the dimness of the room, the low visibility of the space. Not one person had known it was already broken before it was brought into the room.

Well, except for one person keeping his mouth shut…

Voras. He alone knew the truth. If he decided to tell the others, their entire plan would be foiled, which was why they had approached him beforehand.

"I do not mind. It's the role of a leader to aid the youth in their times of trial. Nevertheless, I can only promise that I will do nothing. If you wish for me to react in some way, show me that you can provide an appropriate opportunity."

Voras didn't pry for any more details about their plan.

The real battle was about to begin. Wein had no suggestions to help with what would come next. Felite would have to use his own power to convince both Voras and the other *Kelil* to follow his command.

The battle begins—! Felite took a breath.

"I understand the implications of my actions, Sandia. It will reduce the amount of blood spilled in our future."

"Do you even hear yourself?!" Sandia's expression said he was ready to grab Felite by the collar at any second. "The Rainbow Crown was a symbol! Who can predict the chaos that will befall Patura without it?!"

"Nothing will happen." Felite's voice crackled like fire. "There will be no chaos. Patura has the Zarif. Even without the Rainbow Crown, we will never allow havoc to come to the islands."

"...A bold proclamation," Emelance challenged. "The Zarif lost their former *Ladu*, Master Alois, not to mention their soldiers and wealth. All that's left is you and your small retinue. How can you talk so big?!"

"Because of what we've already managed to accomplish."

Don't give in. Don't cower. Let the winds blow as they please. I've endured that grueling interrogation. I won't complain about something as easy as this.

"Starting with Malaze, the Zarif has ruled over Patura. Each successive generation took on challenges and guided our people. In return, the people accepted the Zarif as their *Ladu*."

"B-but!" Corvino tried to interrupt, but Felite didn't let him.

"We needed it when Patura was trying to unite as a single nation. But now we have years of accumulated accomplishments! Success under the Zarif! Look at our history! Even without the Rainbow Crown, we will not be reduced to nothing!"

The *Kelil* didn't know what to say. Even these men who each had ten or more ships and the seamen to command them were stunned, left breathless before this young man who had lost everything.

"From this moment forward, I will continue our history! I will defeat Legul and lead this inexperienced nation dependent on the godly authority of the Rainbow Crown to a future created by human hands! If you still choose to pursue the shadow of a rainbow, you may leave now!"

The conference room was silent. Only Felite's ragged breathing was audible.

A voice slowly called out.

"...Master Felite." It was Voras. The old veteran had remained silent until then, but he looked at the young leader. "The journey of a trailblazer who has lost the guidance of the gods is grim. If you stray down the wrong path, you take the people with you. That responsibility will be placed onto your shoulders, and the gods will not be there to save you."

"Anyone who cannot bear that responsibility is not fit to be a *Ladu*," Felite responded.

"Heh… I suppose it was foolish of me to even question you." Voras stood from his chair and knelt before Felite. "I, Voras, offer you my sword and helm."

Voras had made his move.

Emelance, Sandia, and Corvino stared at him. A shadow descended, getting on his knee beside Voras.

"I, Edgar, offer you my sword and helm."

Voras cracked a small smile. "I'm surprised someone as stubborn as you is willing to play second fiddle, Edgar."

"I thought I'd want to live my finite life my way."

Of all the *Kelil*, the two veterans had joined Felite's cause. Three remained.

"…Well, that was a short-lived dream."

Corvino spoke up and knelt before Felite, seeing that he had no chance of winning against Voras and Edgar. He'd jumped ship.

"That was splendid, Master Felite. I, Corvino, offer you my sword and helm."

The remaining members, Emelance and Sandia, looked at one another. They had their own motives, and they both knew it.

"Should we follow the rainbow…?"

"I'm not senile enough to chase such fleeting dreams."

"So what do we do?"

"…The rainbow has vanished, but now we have a new path. We're sure to gain something through it."

The two nodded to each other and knelt before Felite.

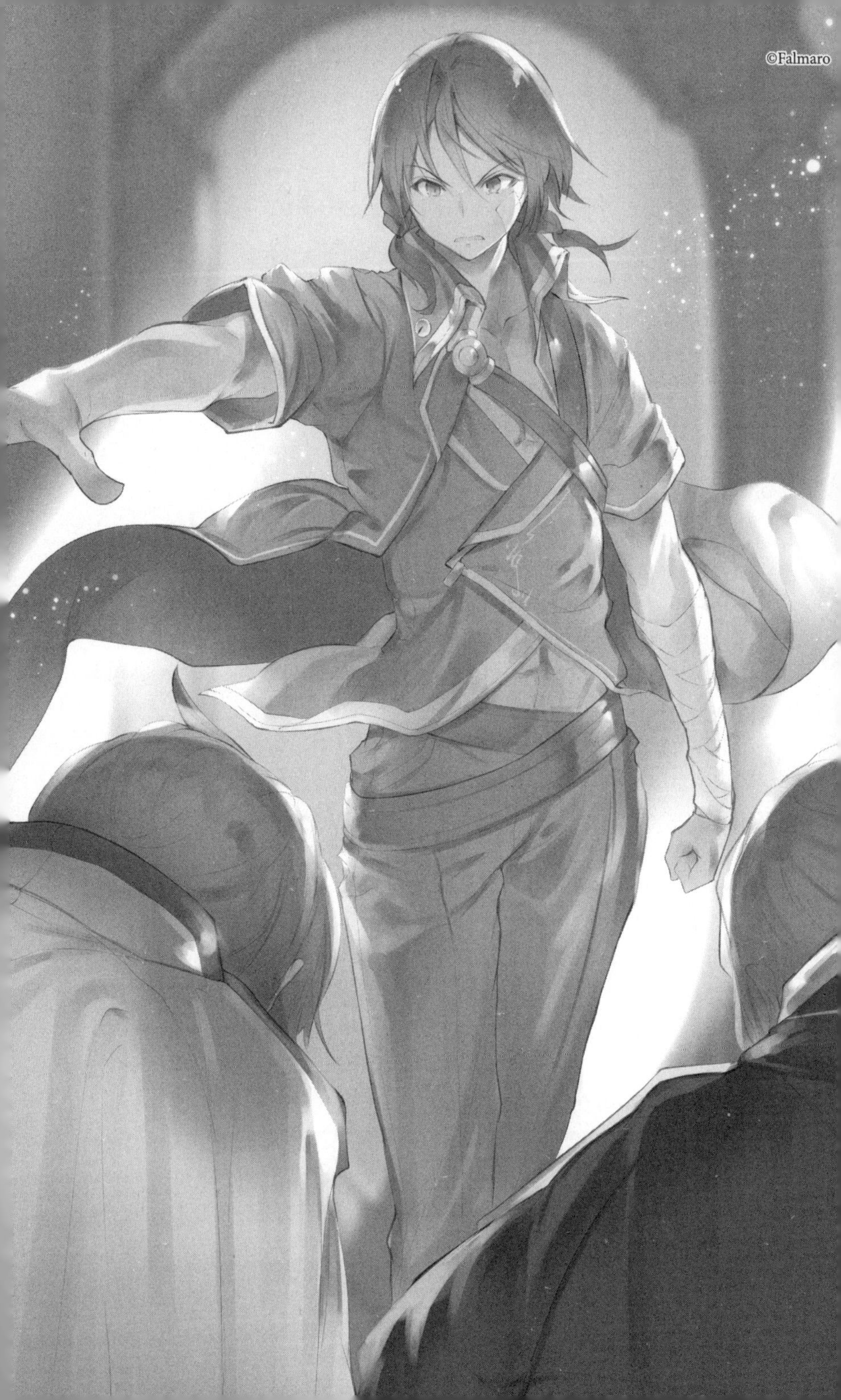

"I, Emelance, offer you my sword and helm."

"I, Sandia, offer you my sword and helm."

Now that he had the loyalty of the five *Kelil*, Felite spoke to all of them.

"The oath here is sealed. All hands, prepare for battle. We'll take down Legul, the murderer of my father, and bring back stability to Patura!"

""—Understood!""

The *Kelil* were on the move.

According to the reports from his spies on every island, at least.

It didn't take long for their activity to reach Legul's ears. It seemed his brother was their ringleader.

"So Felite has the Rainbow Crown."

He didn't know the exact course of events, but he could only assume that was what had led to this current situation.

"……"

Felite was his talentless little brother who had always tagged behind him. Legul had been annoyed by him when they were little, but at the same time, it had made him feel good to have a little brother who openly applauded his gifts.

When had that all changed?

Felite had begun looking at Legul with worry in his eyes. Whenever Legul fought with those around him, Felite had desperately tried to mediate.

It was nauseating. How often had he beaten up his little brother for butting in? It would have been acceptable if he had just fallen in line and stayed silent. Legul would never forgive Felite for trying to give advice.

Now that little brother of his was trying to lead the *Kelil* in a revolt against him.

"He pisses me off..." There was unbridled rage in those words.

The second choice had been selected as successor after Legul was gone, nothing more. Why was Felite getting all cocky? Legul no longer thought of him as his brother. In fact, he would tear him limb from limb with his own two hands.

"—Master Legul."

Just then, a subordinate opened the door to the room.

"What is it?"

The subordinate's voice trembled as Legul stared at him with an open scowl.

"Ah, well, a guest has arrived."

"A guest? Who?"

"Yes, well— Ah."

Another man shoved the messenger in the doorway.

Upon looking at the aristocratic man and his noble, handsome features, Legul rose from his chair.

He was a duke from Vanhelio and a Holy Elite. A great supporter of the arts and known as the Artist Duke. Legul knew his name well.

"Steel Lozzo—?!"

"Hello there. Been a while, Legul." Steel offered a tender smile.

"Why are *you* here...?!"

"No reason. Isn't it normal for a patron to check on those to whom he gives aid?"

Steel seated himself in a chair. Legul watched him in disgust, silently clicking his tongue.

It was the undeniable truth that Steel was Legul's backer. After being banned from Patura, Legul had arrived in Vanhelio, and in this nation facing the sea, he had taken up pirating.

He'd worked to make his comeback, banding with lawless scoundrels to steal boats, attack merchant ships, and amass great power—

But he'd been completely crushed...by this man named Steel right in front of him.

The very memory of it humiliated him. When Legul had been captured and brought before Steel, however, the Duke had said, "*—Your anger has artistic potential."*

After that, Steel had poured money and human resources into him. Legul made no effort to resist. In fact, he didn't see this as a loan. He built up his power with every intention of destroying the man once he took over Patura.

Steel knew what Legul was up to, but he had spared no aid and provided Legul with a fleet of ships.

Legul had no idea what ran through Steel's mind.

The only thing he knew was what the man was here for now.

"Well...it seems we're behind schedule."

"......"

Legul had to acknowledge there was a delay.

He was supposed to have gained control of Patura after he led his fleet in the attack against Alois. With the power of the Rainbow Crown, Legul would have gained control of the *Kelil* and seized the islands then and there.

However, he'd failed to secure the treasure. His brother had gotten away before he spat out its location, and the *Kelil* had unified around Felite while Legul was busy looking for it.

"Don't get me wrong. I'm not blaming you. After all, artists do their best work after the deadline. I'm used to delays. Anyway, is it true that the *Kelil* have all turned against you?"

"...News reaches you quickly."

Legul had sent in reports, but Steel had his own independent sources. There was no question he'd hurried over because Legul was losing and his investments were coming to nothing.

...Damn them all. Legul seethed. This anger was always with him like a loyal companion.

These emotions he'd been unable to control in Patura mixed with the hatred born of his banishment and, ironically, brought him composure. Thanks to that, he'd been able to steadily drill into the subordinates who commanded his other ships the know-how they needed to be like an extension of him.

"I've been planning on taking down the *Kelil* from the very beginning. If they want to strike back with my stupid brother, that's fine by me. It'll save me the trouble of having to crush them later."

"Can you actually do it?"

"Don't underestimate me, Steel. No one can stand against me on the ocean."

"I see. It seems you're confident in your abilities. Your spirit is alive and well," Steel said with a nod. "In that case, my question to you is: What do you intend to do from here on out? Take out the enemy before they're finished preparing?"

"No, I'll wait," Legul answered. "When I first took out Alois and the *Kelil*, I tried to take control of Patura using moderate methods. Some fools saw this as weakness and seemed to use this as a reason to revolt against me. To stop anyone from foiling my plans this time, I have to make sure they know the full range of my powers." He continued. "I'll wait until they're armed and ready. I'll crush them head-on. Everyone will know I am the king."

"...I see."

"Have something to say?"

"Not at all. It seems very like you. I'm intrigued," Steel replied. "If you need assistance, I will do whatever I can. I look forward to seeing you expunge these old ways and build a new dynasty. Ah, that will make a lovely piece of art."

There was a smile on Steel's face, but his expression was utterly monstrous.

Meanwhile, Felite's camp of *Kelil* was preparing for battle. Ships, crew, provisions, people—Felite grew dizzy at the large volume of goods and people being hauled back and forth.

Of course, he would never complain. After all, he knew the possibilities that this rush signified. Legul would make his move if they wasted time. They had to make sure they were as prepared as possible before that happened.

Seeing as they were still human, however, rest was necessary. During these breaks, Felite always visited the library. Several days prior, they had sent people out to recover the documents in the hideout and archived them here. These breaks allowed Felite a momentary respite.

On this day, though, there was a visitor who had arrived earlier.

"Are you taking a break, too, Wein?"

"Ah, Felite."

When Felite entered the library, he spotted Wein sitting among documents spread all around him. Wein and Ninym were outsiders, but they had been put in charge of battle preparations. After all, Felite's men were stretched thin. Since the beginning, the pair had been lending their aid, along with their delegation and the Flahm from the Salendina Company.

"I just finished one of my tasks. I'm sure I'll find something else to do, but I thought I'd kill some time until then," Wein explained.

"I'm surprised you could even finish all those undertakings. I'm so overwhelmed with everything that needs to be done that I came here just to catch my breath."

"Just so you know, there's going to be way more work once you reach the top."

"...I think my decision to dedicate myself to Patura just wavered."

Wein and Felite cracked little smiles.

"What are you reading?" Felite asked.

"The history of Patura. I skimmed it at the hideout, so I thought I'd really read it. I'm finishing up an entry on Malaze."

"Oh, one of my ancestors?"

Wein questioned, "Do you hate Malaze?"

"...It's complicated. If you consider the situation at the time, Malaze's decision to bring forth the Rainbow Crown and seek authority was a wise one."

A century prior, danger had befallen Patura. Another powerful nation from the Eastern continent—one separate from the Empire—had attacked it. At the time, each island had been controlled by a different clan that served their own motives since they were not unified in any sense.

Bemoaning the enemy nations that took advantage of this and slowly encroached on them, Malaze Zarif had taken action. Producing a multicolored jewel out of thin air and calling it the Rainbow Crown that had been granted to him by Auvert, he united the islanders as a messenger of the god. After banishing foreign forces, he reigned as the ruler of Patura and maintained the islands as an independent nation.

"Under the god, the group became one, after failing to form a nation by themselves. You can't deny its powers. Even the fortress that held us captive was built and commanded by Malaze, so he must have had considerable power. However, the truth remains that such origins brought us to this very situation. While I do personally think he's an incredible person, he can be extremely aggravating at times."

Felite flashed a dry smile. "I think it's somewhere in that book. Have you read about it already? About the Rainbow Crown's true form?"

"Yeah, it's in there all right. That it's just a shell."

The Rainbow Crown was in the shape of a spiral seashell. Some said it had been created by a skilled craftsman overlapping layers of jewels. Anyone who got a close look at its brilliance would know its indescribable twinkle was beyond human knowledge. This gave credence to the idea that it was a divine piece of art that had once belonged to Auvert.

There was a theory, however, that it looked like a shell because it really *was* just a shell.

"There's a shellfish called 'anemia' that lives in the waters off the Southern continent. It has the same exact shape as the Rainbow Crown but goes by another name: 'the rock eater.'"

As the alias suggested, anemia consumed rocks in its surroundings, and it would come to be the same color as the digested sediment to hide from predators.

"In other words, the Rainbow Crown is an anemia that grew up eating jewels… Would such a diet change its appearance that much?"

"Some researchers looked into it in the past, but it seems that giving one a fist-sized gem only slightly changes the shell's edges to a jewel tone."

"In that case, that must mean Malaze stumbled upon a huge gem deposit in the ocean where a bunch of anemia were feeding, away from predators…or something like that. Anyone would think that would be a gift from the heavens."

"Absolutely. Malaze must have thought the gods were supporting him…if it's actually an anemia." Felite smiled and continued. "Malaze left behind one secret instruction. It is written in the book…"

"Yeah, I read it. *'When the new body nears its completion, the rainbow slumbering in the artificial eye will emerge.'*"

"One theory says this is where he found the Rainbow Crown. I wish he had just told us the place instead of giving us a riddle."

"If your hypothesis is correct, it houses the deposit of gems. Wouldn't it be reckless to tell us about this mountain of treasure?"

"Ha-ha. You may be on to something."

The two chatted idly, but eyes were secretly watching them from the entrance of the library. Wein's aide Ninym and Felite's servant Apis.

"Master Felite looks like he's having fun…"

"They must get along because they're similar in age and rank."

They had originally arrived ready to tell their masters to return to work, but they'd decided to wait, letting the men enjoy the conversation.

"…Ninym, is Prince Wein someone who laughs often?"

"Huh? Yes. More than when he was younger. These days, he's become quite expressive." Ninym nodded.

"Master Felite is the opposite. I've seen fewer smiles as he's aged."

Now that Apis thought about it, it all led back to his mother's death. Prior to that, Felite had been a bright boy; his smile had almost entirely disappeared on the day he'd lost his mother and brother. His father had been depleted of all strength after losing his wife and successor, hardly paying any notice to Felite, who had become his new heir. Perhaps Alois had abandoned his second son because his seafaring talents didn't compare to Legul's.

Alois's treatment of Felite naturally created distance between the boy and those around him. Like his brother before him, Felite ended up living alone. A dark cloud loomed over him.

However, Felite did not wither away. Day in and day out, he was either polishing his sailing skills or studying documents.

Apis had believed her master's efforts would be rewarded one day. Once he became *Ladu*, she was certain the islanders would recognize all the work he had done. But then the storm of Legul had wrecked his life once again.

Alois died. Felite was captured. She escaped while her master acted as bait, and she failed miserably, letting the Rainbow Crown out of her sight. She asked herself over and over if she should just put an end to herself.

After many twists and turns, her master was accepted by the *Kelil*, allowing him to smile again.

"Ah. I'm happy and a little frustrated. I wanted to be the one to bring back his smile."

Apis didn't mind all that much, though. His meeting with Wein was surely a blessing of the Sea God.

To reward Felite for his long, hard efforts. To support him in his efforts to create history with human hands.

A modest miracle—the first and last of its kind.

"...Our masters are our suns," Ninym said with a smile. "It is our duty to support them from the shadows and ensure their light shines bright. There's no time to be frustrated. Let's both do our best for their sakes."

"Agreed."

Apis nodded, allowing her lips to curl into a small smile.

Felite's forces were ready for battle.

Legul's men were prepared, positioned to approach the enemy.

The final battle between brothers was about to begin.

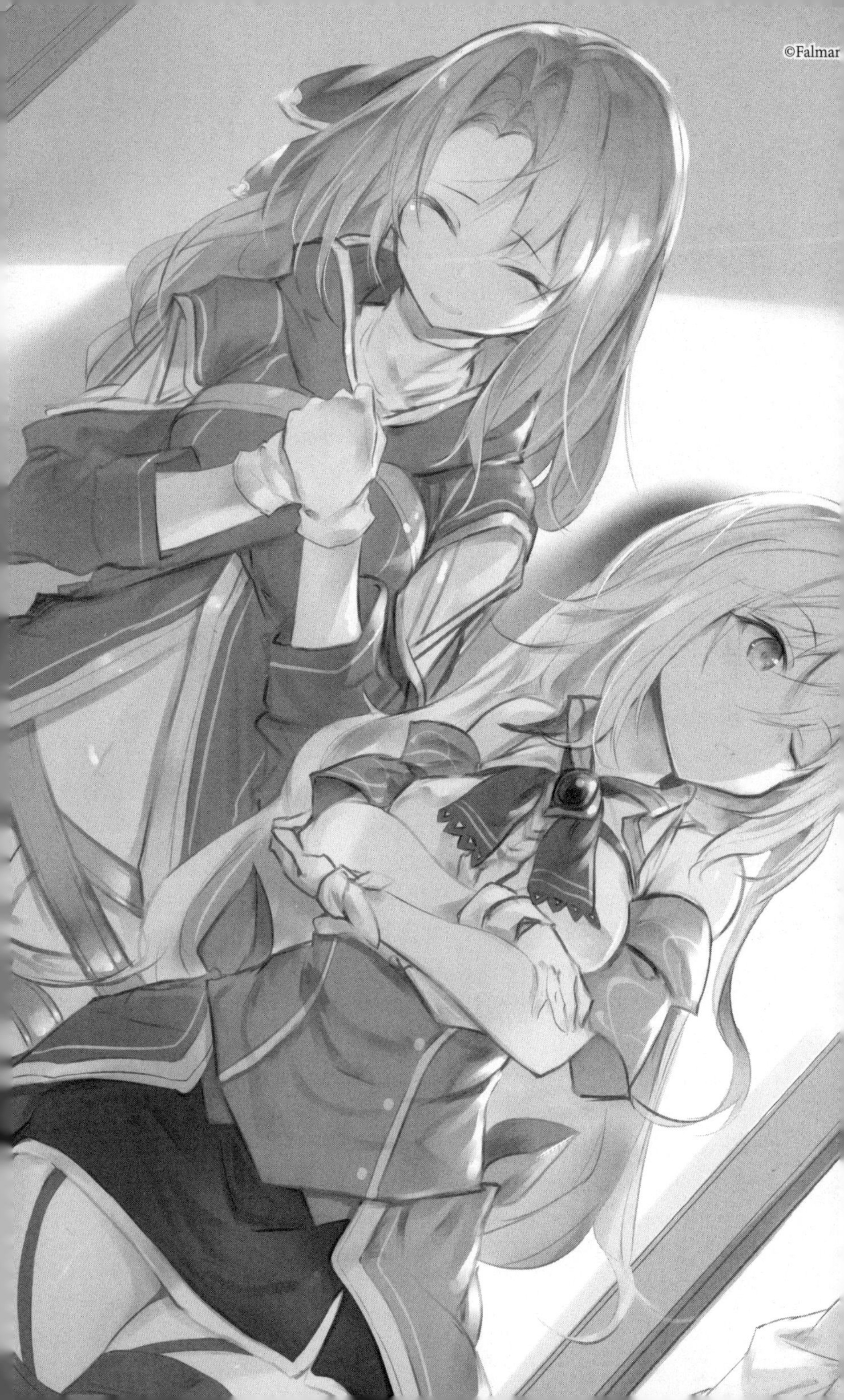

Chapter 5 | At the End of a Rainbow

"Master Legul! Enemy fleet detected!"

"So they're finally here…"

In his captain's cabin, Legul took in his subordinate's report with closed eyes and slowly rose to his feet. He left the room to step onto the deck. The briny air caressed his cheek. There were a few clouds in the sky, but the weather was mostly clear.

A gentle breeze blew from the south, and the waves rolled over the water's surface.

He looked around him, ships in an orderly line, numbering sixty-five. Each was a sailing vessel. They represented almost the entire arsenal in Legul's possession.

Legul's eyes bored into the horizon. Tiny shadows spurted up from the sea.

Ships. All headed his way.

"Forty-five…fifty… They have approximately fifty ships! All galleys!"

The enemy fleet. In other words, Felite's army.

They were almost evenly matched. Based on the information gleaned in earlier investigations, this was the best the *Kelil* could do.

"Do they think they're going to win?"

The victor in this battle would take control of the Patura Archipelago. There would be no tie. One fleet would achieve glory, and the other would die.

"To choose this day for our decisive battle…"

The days had been blustery.

Like Rodolphe, Felite was approaching Legul's core of sailing vessels with an entire fleet of galleys. His younger brother would be at a disadvantage if strong winds roughed up the seas, which explained why he'd chosen to have their final battle on a day when the air was relatively calm. Felite must have been thinking that he'd lose the chance to win if he waited any longer.

"…Pathetic. Doesn't even know what's coming for him," Legul jeered. He raised one hand.

The sixty-five ships began to move, unified.

Legul's fleet sailed into action.

Felite spotted them from aboard his flagship, trembling instinctively.

"Are you nervous, Master Felite?" Apis asked beside him.

Felite nodded. "Yes. I am."

Over a hundred ships would be crashing against one another in one, decisive battle. Battles of such a scale hadn't yet existed in the history of Patura.

"…I thought I would succeed my father after Legul was banished. However, I never had any plans of making a name for myself."

All Felite wanted was for his reign to be peaceful, and yet he was making a name for himself in history books.

"It seems life often does not go as planned," he noted.

"I couldn't agree more."

Felite grimaced. This was unexpected. If he were one of the gods, he could probably avoid this battle altogether and bring back order. As a mere mortal, however, he had no choice but to overcome the trial before him.

"Send word to each of the *Kelil*: We'll follow the plan and see this through to victory."

The battle was going to be a struggle—with a slight advantage on Felite's side.

The basic strategy hadn't changed: striking ships with naval rams and coming alongside the enemy to engage in hand-to-hand combat. To top it off, the wind and waves were gentle, giving the advantage to Felite's galleys.

Emelance, Sandia, and Voras had experience with Legul's fighting style and shared information among themselves. The enemy's sailing vessels were not to be underestimated.

All this put them in an advantageous position. Even so, their small lead could be attributed to Legul's prioritizing defense over offense.

"...He's fighting a war of attrition," Emelance murmured as he commanded his ships.

He had assumed this might happen. If Felite's forces attacked while the wind was weak, the enemy would strengthen its defenses and wait for the wind to change directions.

A war of attrition will be hard on the galleys.

Since the galleys ran on manpower, the sailors had to row with heavy oars. Naturally, extended battles would exhaust the men, dulling their movements. The burden placed on sailing ships was wildly different.

At this rate, we'll need to finish the battle before our fatigue peaks.

Even if it was tiny, an advantage was an advantage. The enemy was taking damage, albeit slowly. Felite's forces would win if this carried on.

That said, Legul wouldn't just take the beating. Emelance considered what the man might be up to.

"The battlefield..." he observed, "is moving southward."

"Armada Five is taking damage!"

"Voras's fleet is in close proximity to the Armada Eleven. They can't budge!"

"The enemy ships aren't slowing down!"

Legul was bombarded with reports of each armada raising up flags of distress. Nearly all of them reported they were being pushed back. However, he wasn't the least bit fazed.

They hadn't even lost ten ships yet. This was because Legul's forces were focused on keeping a safe distance from the enemy, evading its attacks, and staying on the defensive.

If one hundred ships clustered together, they'd end up immobile. The sea would become a congested mess and temporarily turn into a jigsaw of ships. If that happened, the armies would engage in close combat, and even Legul wouldn't be able to tell which way the battle was leaning.

So Legul made sure his ships kept their distance. This would minimize the damage they incurred and give him leeway to change course as needed. This, of course, meant Felite's forces would suffer even less damage—but destroying them wasn't Legul's objective.

"It's almost time."

When Legul ordered his ships to maintain their distance, he'd given one more command: to inch south, pretending they did so to dodge the enemy's attacks.

"They must have realized it's too late now."

Legul had noticed something before the start of the battle. After all, the wind and waves spoke to him.

Something was being carried by the southern winds. Dark, heavy clouds rolled in.

Just like when he'd taken down Alois.

"You've lost, Felite."

A Dragon Storm.

The seasonal tempest arrived on the naval battlefield.

The tide of battle changed in a flash. The Dragon Storm brought forth heavy, pelting rain, and the raging winds drew up violent, crashing waves.

Galleys did not fare well in rough waters. A smooth surface allowed sailors to synchronize their rowing. When the waves spun and seawater splashed in the oar ports, it disrupted their forward momentum.

"Sir Edgar! Ally ships are raising signal flags that they're unable to advance!"

"With the wind and waves, it won't be long before our own ship suffers the same fate!"

"Settle down! We'll do all we can to get through it!" Edgar clicked his tongue as he reprimanded his weakening subordinates. "Rough winds would be hard for even a sailing ship to navigate, but..."

If both sides had fleets made of all galleys, they would have retreated to try again later. However, Legul's fleet of sailing ships used this wind to ram into Felite's galleys. As his forces saw it, the immobile boats made for prime targets. The roles of offense and defense were reversed, and Felite's ships began sinking without any way of even protecting themselves.

"Oh, how he despises us...!"

Legul's flagship wasn't the only one moving through the storm; his fleet of followers had flipped it to their advantage. Just how much genius had he been bottling up, and how well did he train his subordinates? The only thing clear was that he loathed Patura.

"You underestimated us, Legul! Our new *Ladu* will totally disarm you—!"

That's strange, Legul thought.

The storm had given him the advantage. That had been part of the plan.

His opponent's response, however, had been far quicker than expected. The enemy didn't seem to falter, persistently sticking it out. It was as if Felite's forces had known the storm was coming all along.

Ridiculous. There's no way.

Predicting the weather from the wind and waves was not an unusual skill among seamen. No one on this earth, however, pulled it off to the same level of accuracy as he.

Not to mention no one would challenge this type of storm, knowing the weather. None of the enemy ships have sails or masts. They must have realized they have no way of catching the wind.

There were galleys with masts and sails that allowed them to travel along the wind. Felite's ships, however, were run entirely by rowed oars. The lack of extra weight from the masts kept the boats agile.

That's why I didn't think they'd predicted the Dragon Storm. It's why I planned on winning this war by holding out until it arrived. But if the enemy saw it coming—

His opponent could have intentionally forgone the sails and

masts to make Legul think they didn't know about the Dragon Storm and drag him farther onto the battlefield.

"———"

It was idiotic. Impossible. There was no way the enemy had anyone who could read the wind that well. Besides, their efforts were pointless. Felite's ships should be swallowed up by the wind and find themselves at a disadvantage. If the enemy could predict the direction of the wind, it should have been using this knowledge to evade Legul.

He was clearly overthinking things. Legul snapped his head up to look out at the southern sky.

"…What the?"

He read the wind, and his natural genius allowed him to pick up on an anomaly.

"Something's coming…"

Chills ran up his spine. The wind was gusting strongly enough to tear through the sails.

No, it was something else. It was a wave, threatening to swallow the ship whole.

Wait. That wasn't it, either.

Whatever it was, it was almost upon them.

"What is this…?!"

He gaped at the dark cloud squirming across the sky.

"We'll use the Dragon Storm."

In the conference room, Felite spoke to the five *Kelil* and Wein, who was sitting at the head of the table.

"Legul will be able to predict the Dragon Storm, seeing that he's resourceful and used this exact method to carry out his heinous acts toward my father. We'll use this against him."

"...I find that hard to believe," Sandia stated. "The Dragon Storm is a natural phenomenon that comes on a whim. How could even the greatest seafarer predict such a thing?"

"It's entirely possible for that man. His ability to read the wind is uncanny," Edgar replied, expressing agreement with Felite.

The rest of the *Kelil* knew Edgar was not one to exaggerate. They trembled in fear of Legul's power.

Voras asked a question. "Well, then, Master Felite. If we use the Dragon Storm against him, shall we challenge Legul to battle on the day it is to occur?"

Before Felite had a chance to answer, Corvino had an objection. "Wait. If our main force of galleys is caught in the Dragon Storm, we'll be stuck in place."

"That's precisely why we're doing it," Voras replied. "According to our new sources, Vanhelio is standing behind Legul, right? Time is on the enemy's side. We must make them believe that dragging us into a decisive battle will bring them definite victory."

"I see... So we'll engage in battle on the day of the Dragon Storm on purpose and defeat Legul before it arrives," Emelance said with a nod.

Edgar frowned. "I have questions. First, how can we predict the Dragon Storm? Second, how will we be able to defeat Legul before it arrives if that's exactly the opposite of what he wants?"

The sea admirals groaned. The first issue was impossible. The second was hardly more feasible. This strategy didn't seem conceivable by any means.

Felite faced them. "Predicting the Dragon Storm is indeed possible. Two have already occurred while we were preparing for battle, and I successfully sensed them both beforehand."

"What?!"

"When did you learn how to do that?!"

Felite shook his head at the *Kelil*. He took out a thick sheaf of paper.

"It's not a matter of my own ability. By compiling the information in these documents recorded by the Zarif, I was able to analyze omens of the Dragon Storm," Felite admitted. "By sharing these records, many people will be able to recognize precursors of the Dragon Storm. This will increase our accuracy and allow us to decipher the best time to begin the battle."

"I see... Even if we cannot take on Legul on our own, we can as a group," Voras murmured in admiration.

Felite nodded. "There is one more matter to discuss. The objective of this strategy is not to conclude the battle before the Dragon Storm arrives. We'll finish this fight after we overcome this special storm."

"Overcome what special storm...?"

Felite took out a new set of documents and passed them out. "...It was Prince Wein who discovered and compiled these from among the records. I, too, was surprised."

The *Kelil* looked at Wein and then back to the documents. They gingerly thumbed through the papers, eyes growing wider by the sentence.

"This can't be..."

"Do these things seriously happen?"

"Hmm, ah, well..."

They started to stir.

"This is a gamble." All eyes fell on Wein, who flashed a haughty smile. "If this information is correct, all the conditions for a special storm have been satisfied. We can expect one to brew soon. In theory, at least, based off the records."

A gamble. Were they willing to risk hundreds—maybe thousands—of lives for information written on sheets of paper?

"Master Felite, do you believe this to be true?" Edgar asked meekly.

Felite nodded. "Yes, I do," he declared. "The collective history of the Zarif is authentic. And I shall use this battle to prove it—"

"Master Felite!"

"I know!"

Looking out at the unusual sky from his flagship, Felite clenched his hand into a tight, nervous fist.

"There's a peculiar type of Dragon Storm that only comes once every several decades. Omens of its coming include an unusual uptick in windy days, higher temperatures, and plants that bloom earlier than in previous years."

"Sir Corvino! Our ally ships cannot hold any longer!"

"Just a bit more!" Corvino roused his subordinates, glaring at the sky.

"There was something that matches your legends. Auvert uses his golden spear and white-silver shield to take down the sea dragon ravaging the ocean."

"Elemance's ship hasn't sunk yet, right?!"

"Correct, Sir Sandia! The flagship of Elemance's armada is still in good form!"

Eyeing the capsizing ships, Sandia clicked his tongue and let out a sigh of relief.

"There are some myths that are based in truth. That might be the case for these documents here. The sea dragon is an odd storm. The golden spear is the sun's ray that pours down from the sky. The white-silver shield is the surface of the ocean that glares against the sun. These all culminate to create one strange phenomenon."

"These are the perks of a long life," Voras said with a small smile. "I can't say I ever thought I'd witness such a sight."

"——A lull."

The wind died down.

For a moment, Legul couldn't understand what was happening.

The dark clouds overhead dispersed. He could see that much. Although the clouds had cleared, the wind remained. As long as he had that, he would hold the advantage.

Except the wind stilled.

"Damn it... The hell is this?"

The surface of the water reflected the sun's rays, and the previously turbulent sea had calmed. It was as if they were suddenly transported to a new world.

A lull. It was a period when all wind subsided from the sea. Even Legul couldn't have predicted this phenomenon would occur after the Dragon Storm died down.

And if Legul couldn't perceive it, no one in the world could.

Or so he'd thought.

"Master Legul! The enemy fleet is getting ready to attack!"

"Ngh——!" Legul saw them. Now that the storm had abated, the galleys were moving toward each of his armadas. Such a bold move gave him no choice but to assume they had predicted the period of stillness.

If they knew this was coming, that explains their actions! But how?! How did they figure out something that I didn't?!

Legul had no clue. He had never read the documents passed down through generations of Zarif. His talent gave him no reason to even consider it. He therefore had no way of knowing the truth that the knowledge gleaned from the history of the Zarif far surpassed his own skills.

—Be that as it may, even if he was unaware of what was going on, he dealt with the situation and gave his orders.

"Send out a signal flag! All ships are to withdraw from the area!"

Legul was a smug man. His pride made him think twice before turning his back and fleeing from the enemy. His voice of reason, however, stifled the urge to fight until the bitter end. Even now, his resentment gave him a broader perspective.

"We need to fall back! Take out the oars! We'll hide on the small islands behind us and—"

"Master Legul!" cried out one of the subordinates.

"What now?" Legul turned to the man and noticed he was looking behind them. Legul peeled his eyes toward the ocean.

His eyes grew large.

"When the hell did that happen…?!"

In the expanse of ocean, five ships bearing the crest of Natra sailed in as if to blockade them.

"I'm afraid I can't let you go anywhere."

Five ships cruised on the sea. From aboard the flagship, Wein broke into a sassy smile and stared at Legul's fleet.

"To think the battlefield would move this far out to sea," Ninym murmured in surprise next to him.

The five ships under Wein's command had circumvented the ocean since before the start of the battle. The fleet was secretly stationed within the area to keep Legul and his forces from escaping.

"The Dragon Storm always blows from the south upward. Which means the enemy will try to corner us on the battlefield so we get hit with the storm first. If that's how it's going to be, we just need to predict when it'll hit us and hunker down to weather the storm."

Wein made it sound so easy, but Ninym knew it wasn't so simple.

He had to calculate how fast all the forces would move across the entire battlefield and the progression of the developing storm. Plus, he had to hide his ships in the shadows of the nearby islands. She thought to herself that he was a monster.

"…But if you know that much, I would have preferred it if you hadn't climbed aboard yourself and risked the danger."

"Don't be that way. I only did this to see the battle through. I don't think Felite will go back on our agreement or anything, but I'm not sure if we've completely won over the *Kelil*. That's why we need to remind them in an obvious way that Natra was the one who came to their rescue."

"But you're fine with hopping on an escape boat if they come near us, right?"

"Obviously," he said. "There's not a single fighter on these ships."

The five boats held only the bare minimum of sailors—apprentices who had no experience on battleships. Wein had instructed them to

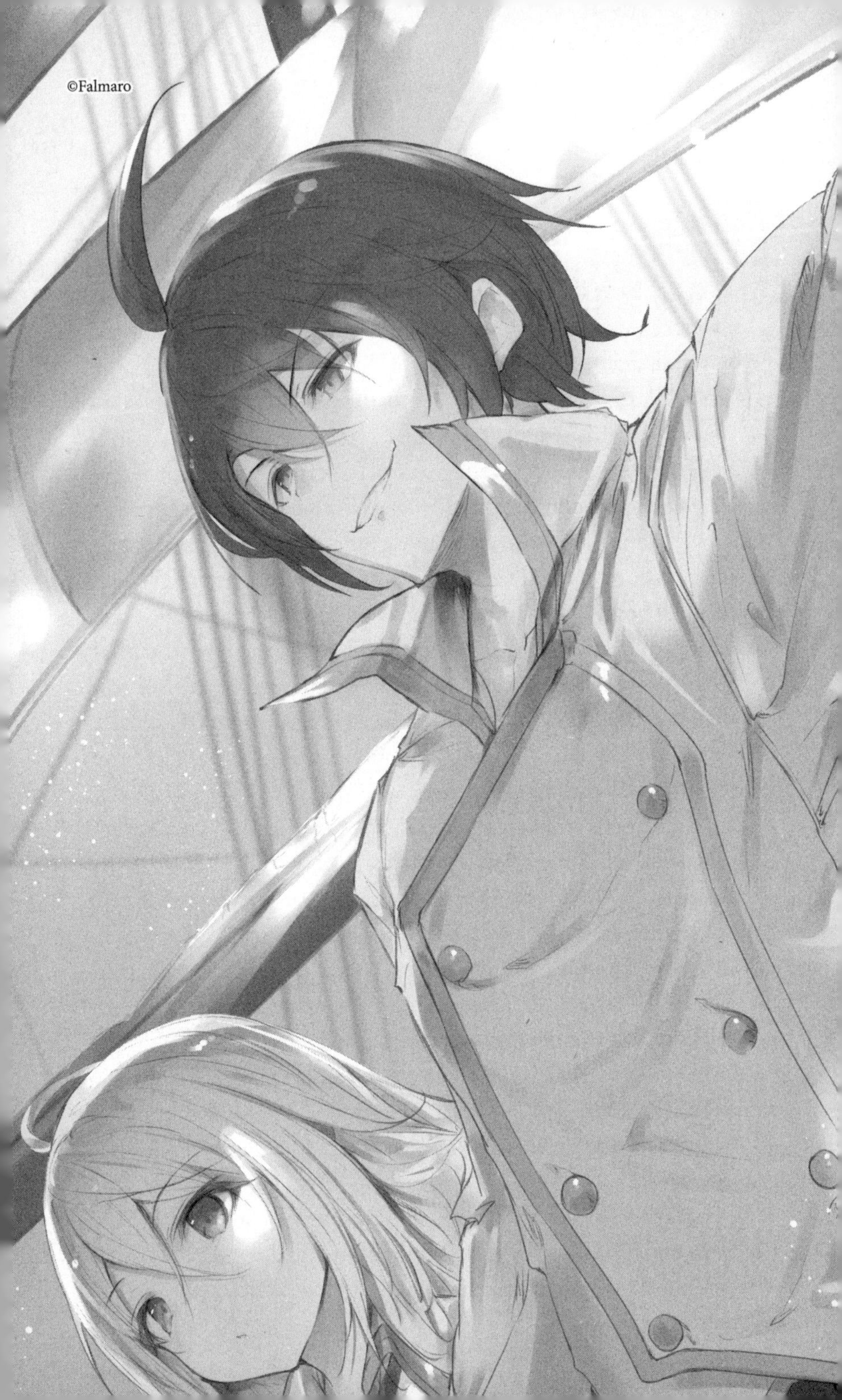

flee if an enemy ship approached. They were there only to contain Legul and nothing more.

"Do you think they've noticed?"

"One would think." Wein grinned. "Knowing you can't avoid something really sucks."

"Calm down! It's just a scare tactic!" Legul called out to his panicking subordinates. "If these were battleships, they would have mobilized them sooner! These are just sailing ships! We won't have any problem passing by them!"

The crew became composed, but his voice reached only as far as the ship he was aboard. The other fleets had become rattled by the sight of the enemy suddenly behind them, failing to recover, and the *Kelil* took advantage of every breach in their defenses.

"Master Legul! Our ally ships are…!"

The galleys went to attack the sailing ships that were now at a standstill. Legul's fleet had some oars on board, but these were meant to aid them when there was no wind or they were coming alongside a dock. The vessels didn't stand a chance against a galley in terms of mobility.

"Grr…! Tell them to hold out! This lull won't last long!"

Legul's senses told him the wind would be returning soon, but the enemy must have been aware of this, too. Would his side really be able to endure?

"The enemy flagship! It's closing in!"

Legul heard his subordinate and looked at the ocean with a start. There he saw a single galley fiercely closing in.

"Felite…!"

Did Felite see this as a perfect opportunity to come calling for the enemy admiral? Now that Legul had lost command over his forces, no one was there to stop Felite's passage.

"Don't think that means you can underestimate me!"

A wind would soon blow from the rear left. One single tailwind.

He'd make it in time. The wind would fill the sails, and he'd just barely be able to avoid the galley crashing into him head-on. After that, he'd just need to use that same gust to retreat.

Five more seconds!

Legul started counting. The boat was coming. Just a little more time...

The wind started to blow.

"Starboard!"

The ship turned to the right, and each sail billowed in the wind.

We made it.

Then before his very eyes was the galley turning its bow toward him as if it had predicted this move all along.

"This isn't how I wanted to catch up to you, Brother—!"

Felite's galley rammed into the side of Legul's sailing ship.

Did we only graze him—?!

The charge had been perfectly timed, but by either the whim of the wind and waves or Legul's stubbornness, Felite's naval ram failed to pierce the hull of Legul's sailing ship—instead carving through its exterior.

In all likelihood, the flank would break soon enough, and the ship would sink. But knowing Legul's skill, there was a chance he'd retreat from the battlefield before that happened.

There's no time to put distance between us and charge again! He'll escape unless I finish him off here!

Quickly determining this to be the case, Felite turned and called out to his crew.

"Throw the grappling hooks! We'll strap ourselves onto their boat and get beside it!"

""RAAAAAH!""

The sailors tossed the hooks over the side of Legul's ship. The enemy crew tried to cut the ropes and shake them off, but the onslaught was so overwhelming that it rendered their moves sluggish. The two ships ended up side by side.

"All hands, draw your swords!" Felite shouted. "Board the enemy ship!"

The men drew their weapons, racing across the deck and boarding the opposing vessel.

"Apis, stay here and take charge!"

"W-wait, Master Felite?!" Apis was left behind, baffled, as Felite jumped onto Legul's ship.

"Where is he…?!" Felite huffed.

The sailors had already begun fighting around him, swords clanging against swords. Felite took in these sounds as he went in search of his target—

"I'm right here."

As soon as Felite turned around toward the voice, a bare blade grazed the tip of his nose.

"Ngh……!" Felite instinctively jumped back, taking him in. The figure of his elder brother, Legul, was standing right there. "Brother…"

"That was something, Felite. I can't believe a stroke of good luck managed to drive my ship into a corner."

Even after all that had happened, Legul wasn't going back on his choice to go through with this. He glared at Felite.

"Did you board my ship to try and keep me here? That was one hell of an idea!"

Legul kicked off the deck. Despite the rocking of the ship, his footing was solid, and he swung his sword at Felite.

"You seriously think you can stop me?!"

"Gah?!" Felite took the brunt of Legul's attack with his own sword.

The two blades clashed, sparks shooting from the friction.

"What's wrong, Felite?! You're coming at me?! —Take that!"

A powerful blow sent Felite flying, blade and all. He tumbled across the deck. When he staggered to his feet, he found blood streaming from his chest. He'd been wounded.

"...It's true that my swordsmanship cannot compare to yours, Brother," he admitted. "You've always been better than me."

The cut stung, but it wasn't deep. That said, Felite would lose if the battle continued much longer. Upon diagnosing the severity of his gash, he gripped his sword. "However, I am not just trying to keep you here. I have come to settle things by my own hand, Brother."

"You'll end up dying here for nothing. How pathetic." Legul smiled scornfully.

Felite gasped for air. "...Don't you think it is you who are pathetic? Do you honestly believe you can run from the *Kelil*? You still refuse to give up?"

"Obviously!" Legul answered proudly. "You think we can end things here?! That my resentment will just go away?! I'll keep coming back—every time! And then Patura and the Rainbow Crown will be mine!"

"......" Felite seemed to mourn for Legul. He opened his mouth, saying nothing and then closing it. "Brother...there's one thing I need to tell you."

"What?"

"I *broke the Rainbow Crown* myself."

Legul stopped moving.

They could hear the battle continuing around them, but the two looked at each other as if they were the only people in the world.

"What…did…you…say…?"

"There is no longer anything you desire in this land—or continent."

"…Like hell! Why would the Rainbow Crown ever fracture?! It's Patura itself, passed down by the gods!"

"It's not! It's just a normal shell! Besides, no one needs it anymore! Please open your eyes! The old you had set your eyes on a better future!"

"Shut up! Shut up! Shut up! I've had enough! Talking with you is a waste of my time! All I have to do is kill you all and uncover the Rainbow Crown!"

Legul readied his sword. Nothing was more bloodcurdling than this situation.

Felite could feel a murderous rage radiating from his body.

Words would no longer reach his brother. Felite steeled himself, stabilizing his sword.

Tensions mounted. They didn't break eye contact or breathe, waiting for the perfect moment. And then…the creaking side of the boat that had taken the brunt of the attack started to split.

The two launched themselves off the deck simultaneously.

The body of the ship exploded.

The spray of waves rained down between them.

Two human shadows, two swords, closed in faster than wind to take life, and—

"""_____"""

There was a momentary illusion born from the mist and sun.

Legul's eyes caught sight of the rainbow. Felite's eyes looked beyond it.

Felite's sword sliced cleanly through Legul's body.

Legul looked down at the sword running through him with emotionless eyes.

It felt like the wound was on fire as his arms and legs lost all heat.

I'm dying, he thought. His sword slipped from his hand.

When he looked up, the rainbow was still there. He reached out to grab it, but it vanished before his fingers could touch it.

Come to think of it… He did the same thing when he was little.

How long ago had it been? Legul remembered scolding his brother and telling him to stop doing such stupid things.

Then a memory from that time burst in his mind like a bubble.

"Do you hate rainbows, Brother?"

"*Uh-huh. I'll never forgive rainbows—or the Rainbow Crown—for drawing all the attention away from me. When I'm ruler of Patura, I'll smash the treasure to pieces.*"

"*But everyone will get angry!*"

"*All I have to do is become a man who's worth more than the Rainbow Crown. Just you wait, Felite. I won't stop at Patura; I'll control every body of water across the continent and see what lies at the far ends of the ocean!*"

Felite's eyes had shone as he oohed and aahed. "*Please take me with you!*"

"*Only me and the best of the best can sail on my ship. You seriously think I'd let you aboard?*"

"*Then I'll become the bestest, too! I'll be a great seaman worthy of your ship!*"

"*Hmph. You don't have a chance.*" Legul mocked him, then lowered his voice to a whisper. "*Well, if that does happen, I guess I'll consider it.*"

That was as far as the memory went—just a meaningless reel of the past.

After all, their paths had parted long ago.

"Master Felite! Please return here quickly!"

His brother's subordinate was yelling something. Seawater had begun pouring into the gaping wound on the ship. It would sink soon.

"Brother…" Felite raised his head.

Were his cheeks wet from the spraying seawater?

It didn't really matter.

"—Do you seriously think you've caught up to me?" Legul grabbed the nape of Felite's neck. His hand pressed into his skin. "You idiot. You'll have to train for another century before you can step foot on *my* ship."

"Bro—"

Felite's body sailed overboard.

At that same moment, the sailing vessel began to sink. The galley fighters jumped back to their ship in droves.

Legul Zarif went down with the vessel, and he never rose back up from the waters again.

In the end, Felite Zarif's forces were the victors in the naval battle that saw the mobilization of over one hundred ships, and he took care of any remaining resistance, working side by side with the *Kelil*.

Felite Zarif regained control of the central island, ruling as the leader of the Patura Archipelago.

✠ Epilogue ✠

Two weeks had passed since the Naval War of Patura.

Felite was in the fortress that had once held him as a prisoner—not in a jail cell, but in the command room. The same one his brother used to use.

He had a mountain of work set out for him: mend public relations to encourage others besides the *Kelil* to accept him as the new *Ladu*, rekindle trade with foreign nations, compensate victims of rampant pillaging, suppress the resistance that continued even after Legul's defeat, and other unavoidable matters that made his head hurt.

A knock came at the door.

"Sorry to bother you."

It was Wein. Felite smiled at the friend he'd met through a strange twist of fate.

"Ah, Wein. How can I help you?"

"It's nothing much. Just wanted to let you know we're pretty much packed up and ready to head home," Wein replied. "I gotta get back to my own country. It's been a long trip, but now we've done what we needed to do."

"I see… I cannot thank you enough. I vow I will fulfill our promise one day."

"Thanks. I appreciate it… Can you come with me for a second? There's something I want to show you."

"What could that be?" Felite tilted his head and obediently followed Wein out of the room.

"Your ancestor Malaze made this fortress, right?"

"Yes. A large-scale military port became necessary when he stirred up trouble with other nations. You might say that, in a way, it is a symbol of unity. But what of it?"

"You'll know soon enough."

They headed out of the fortress and finally arrived at a yard for holding goods. Ninym was there.

"We've been waiting for you, Your Highness."

"Is it over there?"

"Yes. I confirmed it earlier."

Wein motioned to an old, unused well. It wasn't for drinking water. Felite remembered it was excavated for seawater to be used during yard fires. The water, however, hadn't pooled in the borehole, and it had been abandoned since.

Whatever it was that Wein wanted to show him, it seemed to be in there.

"Let's go."

"W-wait. What in the world is in there?"

Wein returned a question for a question. "Felite, what's on top of a backbone?"

"Huh?"

Wein climbed down the well with a ladder Ninym had prepared. Felite looked at her, and she gestured—*After you*—urging him to descend.

"...Okay, here goes nothing!"

He couldn't say he didn't trust the motley pair. Felite entered the well.

There were torches fixed to the walls, so the inside wasn't pitch-black. Ninym must have prepared these, too.

This only added to Felite's confusion. Oddly enough, Wein had disappeared from sight.

"Um, Wein—?"

"Over here." A hand popped out from the wall.

Well, not exactly the wall. Though nearly invisible, there was a narrow path for people to walk through at the bottom of the well.

"Wh-what's this…?"

Arriving at the base, Felite let go of the ladder in surprise. *Splsh.* He landed in a puddle of seawater on the ground.

"You'll understand once you solve the riddle I just gave you." Wein took a torch from the wall and started down the passage.

Felite's mind raced as he followed after him.

That riddle.

"What's on top of a backbone?"

On top of a backbone… I guess that would be…a head?

Felite was rubbing his skull when a flash of inspiration came upon him.

"It—it can't be…"

"The trick is to think of the 'top' as something that points north." Wein smiled. *"'When the new body nears its completion, the rainbow slumbering in the artificial eye will emerge.'"*

Words left behind by Felite's ancestor, Malaze. It was said that this riddle would lead to the location of Patura's greatest treasure.

"'The new body' refers to the celestial body of the moon. And 'completion' refers to its waxing and waning. It indicates the flow of the tide."

It would be a full moon tonight, which meant the tide was low. Now that Felite thought about it, the walls and floor of the passage were wet. It was as if they'd been filled with water not long before.

"'The artificial eye.' The eye is in the head. And the head is on top of the spine. In other words, the Patura Archipelago is lying on top of the Giant's Backbone, which cuts the main continent into East and West. That's the head: Patura."

Felite's heart raced a mile a minute. They were drawing near the end of the pathway.

Could it really be? Was it really here?

"And 'the artificial eye' points to a man-made object, located exactly where the eyes are located on the head. Like this fortress, for example."

Malaze had commanded the military port to be built. If there was another reason for its creation… If the fortress above was meant to mask what was buried below…

"—We're here."

Their destination filled Felite's vision.

A room packed from floor to ceiling with gemstone deposits that winked in the torchlight.

"…I can't believe it."

Every ounce of strength left him. He fell to his knees. They grew damp from the seawater, but he didn't care.

"Legul, what you wanted so badly was right here the whole time…"

Shellfish were moving in the water. Anemia.

Their shells shone in rainbow colors. Perhaps Malaze had brought and raised young shellfish here, or maybe they had found their way in and come to live peacefully in this room absent of natural predators. Felite didn't know the answer, but it didn't really seem to matter.

"What will you do?" Wein picked up one of the shellfish at his feet, and it snapped closed on itself. He prodded it with his finger. "You're in a postwar struggle for dominance, right? With these, that power can be yours."

Wein was right. If Felite had the Rainbow Crown, getting people to follow him would be simple.

In fact, it would be all too easy. However…

"I did not become *Ladu* to take the easy way out."

That was Felite's answer.

"I see." Wein gently returned the shell to the water.

"I know I've already asked much of you, but I have one more request," Felite said.

"You want me to keep quiet about this place, right? Sure. Patura isn't my country, after all."

"…Thank you." He bowed. "Let's seal this place off so neither I nor anyone else can obtain the Rainbow Crown. If my heart wavers, I have no doubt that I will try to fall back on its powers."

Wein said nothing. His job now done, he gave a satisfied nod and turned on his heel.

"Well, shall we head back?"

Behind him, Felite called out, "Please wait, Wein. There's something I've been meaning to ask. Now is the perfect time."

"What is it?"

"—Did you break the Rainbow Crown on purpose?"

It had all been an accident. At the time, he'd been so sure. But Felite found himself wondering if it had truly been a coincidence.

"You thought the Rainbow Crown alone wouldn't be enough to persuade the *Kelil*," he continued. "Even I would not be forgiven if I destroyed the crown. You anticipated Rodolphe's boat being below us. If you had dropped it in the ocean, I would have dived after it."

"……"

"The loss of the Rainbow Crown forced me to make a decision. I believe I've grown as a person. Perhaps you had calculated that, too."

"…If that were the case, would it be a problem?"

Felite shook his head. "Not at all. It's just one more thing that I owe you for."

Wein nodded. "It's over. You're not going to chase the shadows of the rainbow anymore, right?"

Felite chuckled. "…No. Let's go back. There's still much to do."

Several days later, Wein left for Natra with a grand send-off.

From then on, the Kingdom of Natra and the Patura Archipelago would enjoy a long friendship that spanned generations.

Only future historians would know how long their bonds lasted and how deep their relations become.

A man sat in a dimly lit room. A canvas was in front of him, his hands holding a paintbrush and palette. He slowly stroked the brush, letting the white canvas become dyed with color. The paintbrush began to speed up, and—

"——Why?!" He smacked both brush and canvas to the floor in anger.

"Why can't I paint?! I've been moved to the core! The natural genius gained nothing and suffered defeat at the hands of the derided younger brother! It was pure poetry!"

The man stomped on the canvas before looking up at the ceiling.

"Oh Lord! Why are you preventing me from becoming an artist?! If you would allow me even one painting—one simple painting—that I alone can create, I would be saved by your grace!"

God did not answer his pleas. Instead, a small voice came from behind the man.

"It appears your wish was not granted, Sir Steel."

A delicate light crept into the darkness. There sat a woman draped in robes.

"Ah...Lady Caldmellia." The man—the Holy Elite Steel Lozzo—caught his breath and faced the woman. "I'm embarrassed to have shown myself in such a state of discomposure."

"Think nothing of it. Indeed, there is no shame in expressing one's suffering. After all, most answers come not from within oneself but from the outside."

"I see. I'm sure that's true," Steel said with a lifeless smile.

"So what will you do? About Patura, that is," Caldmellia clarified.

"Unfortunately, Felite Zarif has completely seized power. It seems he's on good terms with the *Kelil*, so it will take time to rip them apart." Steel continued. "From the impressions of my messenger, he plans to follow in his predecessors' footsteps and remain neutral in the relations between the Eastern and Western regions of the mainland. To be frank, one might call the plan a failure."

The Kingdom of Vanhelio, where Steel lived, had devised a scheme to gently win over the Patura islands by supporting Legul and raising arms against any opposing nations. The only problem was that Legul had been defeated and Vanhelio's aid had come to nothing.

"This is troubling..." Caldmellia noted with a melancholy sigh. "Natra to the north, Mealtars in the center, Patura to the south... Three nations that support the main road connecting East and West. Chaos will never spread like this."

Steel nodded. "Natra has shown breakneck progress. Even King Gruyere admits Prince Wein is powerful."

"Yes... I'm developing a number of plans—some of which involve that nation. However, Prince Wein is keenly perceptive, so I'm curious how many he'll undermine. It's vexing."

"You say that, Lady Caldmellia, but you seem to be rather enjoying yourself."

"Oh dear." Caldmellia pressed a hand to her flushed cheek. "I'm embarrassed for showing girlish giddiness beyond my years. I must apply myself properly and devise a plan that causes the people of the continent to lose everything."

"Loss is one method of unleashing human emotion. I shall help you to my fullest capacity."

"Very well. There appears to be trouble brewing in the East, so let us do our best together to fan the flames of war—"

In the darkness, the two monsters sowed the seeds of tragedy.

No one knew at what point that dark flower would bloom.

"We're hoooome."

Willeron Palace in the Kingdom of Natra.

Wein sighed as he sat in his familiar office chair. The journey had started out with a meeting to conclude a trade deal; instead, he got twist after twist after twist. He'd gained some things in the process, but he still wasn't used to traveling by sea and needed a serious break.

I'll take care of most of these documents before I take some time off.

Wein looked down at his own knees.

"—And what might you be doing, Falanya?"

His little sister was perched on top of them.

"Don't mind me. I'm just sitting here."

"Uh, well, it's hard *not* to mind."

"Don't worry about it."

"Okay."

Falanya seemed to be miffed that she hadn't been included in the long journey. As her big brother, Wein needed to be on his best behavior.

"So, Wein, how was your trip?"

"Huh? Yeah, it was pretty interesting."

"Hmph."

Shoot. That *hmph* meant she was in a bad mood. Wein immediately realized his mistake.

"W-well, why don't the two of us take a trip next time?" Wein blurted out to appease her, but Falanya eyed him suspiciously.

"…Our kingdom's representative will go with little old me on a trip? Just the two of us?"

"Ha-ha-ha. Have some faith in your big brother, Falanya."

"……"

Darn. She didn't believe a word of it.

A younger Falanya might have fallen for his sweet words. He guessed this spoke of her maturity. Speaking of which, he could tell she'd gotten heavier.

"Wein, did you just think something incredibly rude?"

"N-nope! I'm always your perfect big brother!"

"Hmph."

Her ability to read these subtle signs seemed to have heightened. Wein shuddered with the realization. His little sister had become someone not to be taken lightly.

"…Well, it's fine. I'm just happy you're back safe."

"Falanya…"

"By the way, where's Tolcheila? I feel like I haven't seen her since you returned."

"Oh, she went to report to King Gruyere. It seems she'll be there for a while."

"—In other words, I can have you all to myself." Falanya's mood instantly brightened as she broke into a happy smile. "Tell me everything that happened on the islands."

"E-everything?"

"Yes. Knowing Tolcheila, I imagine I'll have to hear her bragging about every last detail. So let me get the jump on her and find out ahead of time…!"

His sister seemed riled up. An indescribable look bubbled up on Wein's face.

If it would make her happy, he figured it was an easy enough task.

"Go ahead, Wein."

"There's a lot to cover. For example—I was in jail."

"Huh?"

"I raised my own ransom to two hundred thousand gold coins."

"What?"

"I smashed Patura's most valuable treasure."

"What in the world have you been up to, Wein…?!"

"Plenty. Well, then, I'll make sure I don't leave out a single detail."

As one might expect, it took a long time to cover everything. Wein finally had some time to take it easy, so he was glad he could spend it with his little sister.

A knock came at the office door.

"Pardon me, Your Highness." Ninym presented Wein with a missive. "We've recently received word from our spies in the Empire."

"…I've got a bad feeling about this."

"Same," Falanya piped up.

If it was about the Empire, he couldn't just dismiss it. Wein opened the letter, Falanya peeking into its contents.

His jaw went slack in surprise.

"—They're having a coronation ceremony in the Empire?"

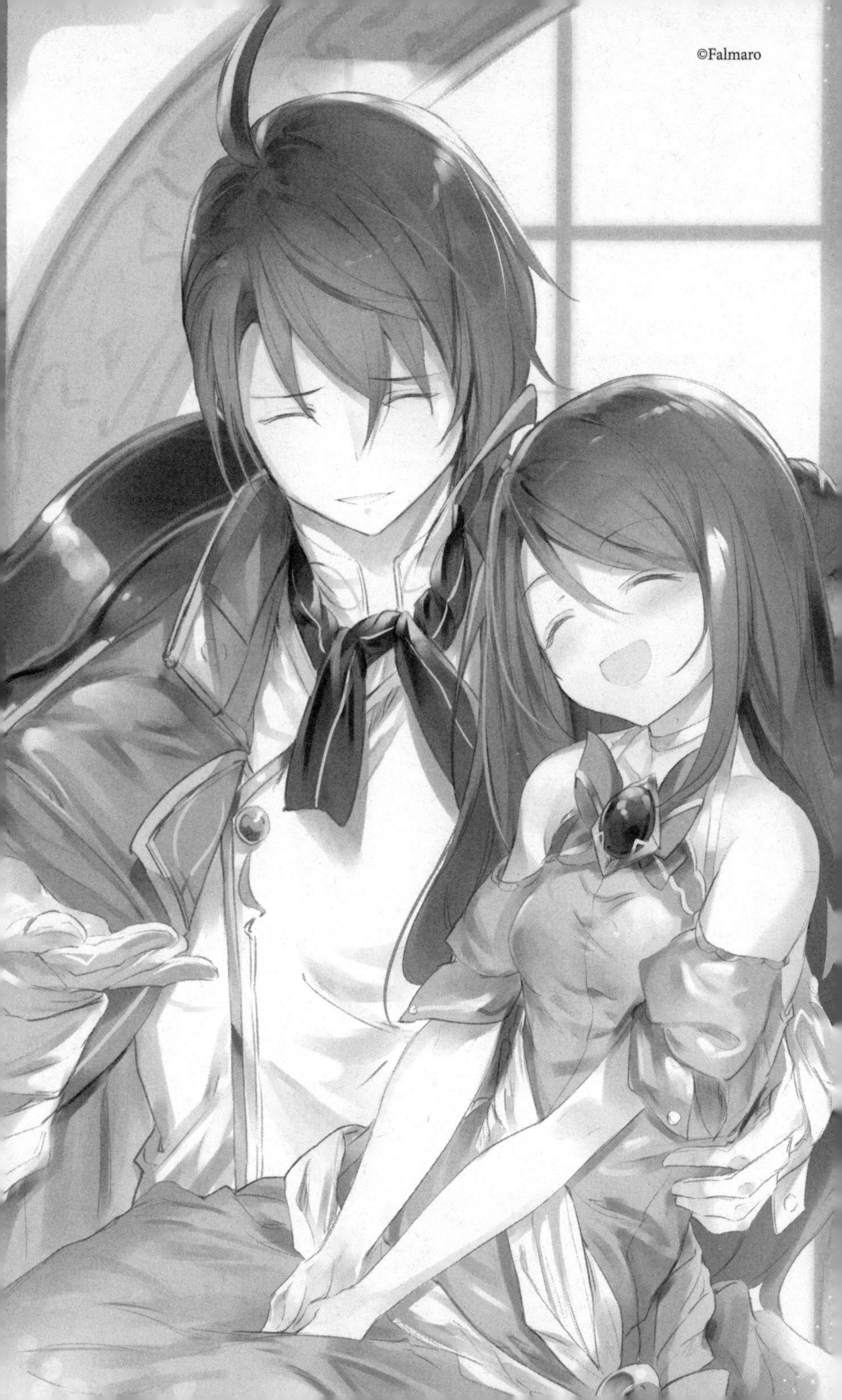
©Falmaro

*   *   *

A new year marked the beginning of a new friendship between the Kingdom of Natra and the Patura Archipelago following a series of complicated events.

It wouldn't be long until the continent of Varno found itself embroiled in new trouble...

Afterword

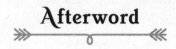

It's been a while. It's Toru Toba. Thank you for picking up the sixth volume of *The Genius Prince's Guide to Raising a Nation Out of Debt (Hey, How About Treason?)*.

The main motif of this volume was the sea! We see Wein shipped off to the tropical islands of Patura from the port that he won from the Soljest Kingdom in the previous volume. I hope you'll enjoy seeing Wein out of his element in a new land that's influenced by neither the East nor the West.

That's it for the sixth volume.

I have to apologize for one thing. I promised in the previous volume to write a slice of life, but that didn't end up happening. I'm sorry for not keeping my promise…!

I found it hard to write around an unfamiliar theme. I just couldn't get the words out. In the end, I decided to continue the main story… To all the readers who were looking forward to it, I'm very sorry.

It might be some time before I get to write something fluffy and wholesome… I still want to write more about the characters' daily lives and school days! I just ask for your patience.

Some thanks are in order.

First, to Ohara, my editor. I'm so sorry for putting you in such a tough position with this volume. Seriously. From the bottom of my heart. I'm going to reflect on my actions… (I guess I say that every volume…)

Thank you to my illustrator, Falmaro! I couldn't get enough of the wardrobe changes and the bathing suits for Ninym and Wein in this tropical climate. I'm already thinking about how I can incorporate swimsuits into every plot of mine…

I would like to thank the artist in charge of the manga adaptation—Emuda. It's been awesome seeing the crew in manga form! They're so cute! The story is approaching the latter half of volume one, and I'm looking forward to seeing how those scenes are rendered in the comic!

I would like to share some exciting news. We're going to publish the first volume of the manga and the sixth volume of this novel at the same time! So please go and check out the manga, too!

Last but not least, I'd like to thank my readers for cheering me on. You made this volume possible. It looks like we might make it to volume 10! I hope you'll support both the novel and the manga from here onward!

For the next volume, I think we'll head back to the Empire. The fight for succession continues to rage, so I hope you look forward to seeing what sort of trouble Wein causes next.

Signing off. I'll see you in the next one!